DARCIE'S DILEMMA

Things haven't been easy for Darcie Killengrey, left with the responsibility of her troubled teenage brother Ross and a past of unhappiness and heartbreak. And then Jake Belfast strides back into her life, as acerbic and contrary as he is exciting and handsome. Having parted on bad terms two years previously, they are forced to work in the same place, and find themselves struggling to put the past behind them. Meanwhile, Ross falls under a dangerous influence that looks set to make Darcie's problems with Jake pale into insignificance . . .

Books by Sue Moorcroft
in the Linford Romance Library:

WHERE THE HEART IS

SUE MOORCROFT

DARCIE'S DILEMMA

Complete and Unabridged

LINFORD
Leicester

First published in Great Britain in 2012 by
Choc Lit Limited
Surrey

First Linford Edition
published 2019
by arrangement with
Choc Lit Limited
Surrey

A catalogue record for this book is available
from the British Library.

ISBN 978–1–4448–4100–8

Published by
F. A. Thorpe (Publishing)
Anstey, Leicestershire

Set by Words & Graphics Ltd.
Anstey, Leicestershire
Printed and bound in Great Britain by
T. J. International Ltd., Padstow, Cornwall

This book is printed on acid-free paper

1

Darcie didn't scream when figures ran across her garden in the inky evening and one pressed his face against the kitchen window, puffing out his cheeks like a bug-eyed, fish-faced monster. She just went on stirring the curry on the hob. 'Yes, Ross, you're so pretty.'

The monster burst through the back door and into the brightness of the kitchen, hands plugged into the kangaroo pocket of his hoodie. 'Dinner smells great.'

The sauce was thick and bubbling, the rice almost at its peak of fluffy perfection. 'It's nearly ready. Hi, Amy,' Darcie called to the smaller figure hovering behind Ross in the doorway. Ross had been 'with' Amy for the last few weeks and, mega commitment in the lives of fifteen-year-olds, had asked if it was OK if he brought her home to share Darcie's signature dish of Thai curry.

1

Flicking his hair from his eyes, Ross pulled the small figure into the light. 'It's not Amy. She went off in a stress, so I brought Casey McClare. This is my big sister, Darcie, Case.'

'Oops, hi, Casey.' Darcie shot Casey an apologetic smile. Casey looked back through black make-up and quills of long, dyed-black hair striped with cobalt blue. Three rings glittered from her eyebrow and her stretchy black dress was a second skin. From Ross's hungry expression, Darcie had a good idea what might be stressing Amy.

Ross dragged his attention back to Darcie. 'Why four places at the table? Who's coming?'

'Just Kelly.'

Ross pulled out a chair for Casey. 'Kelly's been Darcie's bezzy mate since school.' He pulled a soppy face.

'And here she is,' Darcie observed as her friend, after a perfunctory knock, breezed in in her usual flurry, discarding her jacket, smoothing her flyaway hair, plonking a bottle of red wine in

2

the middle of the kitchen table. 'Sorry I'm late. An email from Jake dropped into my inbox just as I was coming out and I couldn't resist reading it.'

'That's nice. You're not late, you're bang on time.' Darcie dropped her eyes to the steaming colander of rice as Kelly said hi to Ross and was introduced to Casey. She would not blush just because Jake's name was in the room. He was Kelly's brother and she talked about him a lot. Darcie had had two years to perfect appropriate, politely interested responses. She'd never told Kelly about what had happened because she didn't want to put Kelly in the position of having to take sides or feeling awkward and, anyway, what *hadn't* happened had rendered confession pointless.

Kelly reached down wine glasses from a cupboard. 'Quite chatty, for Jake. Sounds a bit jaundiced about that posh spa he works at in the Black Forest, and the celebrities who slink off there when they need to be slathered in mud or wrapped in seaweed to cope with fame and fortune.'

Ross looked up. 'Does he really meet celebrities, your brother? I don't remember him much. He hasn't lived in Bettsbrough since Darcie moved back in here, has he?' A shadow flickered across his face.

'No, he lives in Germany.' Dropping into a chair, Kelly picked at the seal on the wine bottle. 'He certainly does meet celebs, at the spa, but he'll never tell you which ones. Anyway, you can renew your acquaintance, next week. He's coming home for a couple of weeks and I've invited him to Darcie's party.'

Darcie dropped the colander. Steaming rice poured into the sink and over the worktop. 'Oh, shit!' she muttered.

*　*　*

Ross loved his sister, he really did. Living with her was cool. But the way that Darcie's assessing blue eyes kept resting on Casey during dinner made him uncomfortable. It didn't help that Casey had gone all quiet as if Darcie was the enemy, even though Darcie had spoken normally to her and most of Ross's friends thought she was pretty cool. 'I'm going to walk Casey home,' he said, when he'd eaten a vast portion of curry, plus seconds, and Casey seemed to have finished with the modest portion she'd eaten about half of.

Darcie just smiled, 'OK.' It was Kelly who wagged a mock-admonishing finger behind Casey's back. She'd known him since he'd made his entrance into the world when she and Darcie were already in senior school, and had no hesitation in embarrassing him.

Ross just opened the back door to let Casey through, grinning at her. She smiled back. Her lips seemed somehow to draw together in the centre, even as they curled up at the corners. He wondered how Casey would react if he took her hand. As if in answer, she folded her arms as they strolled through the early summer evening towards her estate, Blossom End, and Ross had to content himself with letting his arm brush against her shoulder as they walked.

Darcie's house and Blossom End stood on the crest of opposing rises. The route between lay along Queen's Road, bisecting Peterborough Road at a busy intersection in the dip, and becoming King's Road.

They crossed the intersection, not waiting for the pedestrian lights but dodging the traffic, laughing when a small blue van beeped angrily. Halfway up the King's Road hill, Casey halted. 'See you, then.'

Surprised, Ross halted, too. 'Don't you want me to walk you the rest of the way?'

She shook her head.

'Oh. OK.' He shuffled his feet, taking out his phone to check the on-screen clock. If he'd known he was going to be blown off by half eight, he wouldn't have suggested they left Darcie's so soon after dinner.

'Your Darcie doesn't like me.' Her dark eyes were speculative.

Ross switched his gaze to Casey. From his vantage point he could see about five millimetres of hair either side of her parting was brown instead of black. Her words prickled. Somehow, it would've been OK if he'd still been living with Mum and Dad and Casey had been negative about his mum. He supposed he'd treated mother love pretty casually — though he wouldn't now, given the chance. But big sisters? Well, they didn't have to change their whole lives, to sell their own place and move back into the family home when your parents died. But Darcie had.

He made his voice bored. 'Is this where I'm supposed to reassure you that Darcie, and everyone else on the planet, adores you?'

She ducked her head to peep at him through her hair. Then grinned. 'Good. You get me.'

Congratulating himself that he hadn't let her wind him up, he grinned back. 'Darcie's cool. She likes pretty much everybody.'

★ ★ ★

Kelly had already gone home and Darcie was sprawled on the sofa enjoying the last of the red wine when Ross slouched in. She put down her book and he took the vacant space on the sofa beside her with his usual ungentle bounce landing. 'You're soon home. Doesn't Casey live far away?'

Ross took his phone out of his pocket and checked the screen, something he did every few minutes, like a nervous twitch. 'Blossom End.'

Darcie felt her eyes narrow. Blossom End was a notorious warren of houses and walkways built in the sixties, generally considered a no go area for non-residents of its forbidding streets. 'You've been walking around that place on your own?'

Ross shrugged. 'She lives on the edge, near King's Road, it's not too bad.'

Darcie felt one of those bumps in her chest that came when Ross said or did something to worry about. Blossom End. Market towns weren't meant to have sink estates but Blossom End pretty much fit the profile.

He withdrew one hand from his pocket, holding a stick of chewing gum. 'Share a chewy?'

'You have it.' But Darcie smiled, aware that the offer was a gesture of deep affection.

He examined the wrapper as he peeled it off. 'I think Casey's family's a bit whatitsname — dysfunctional. She just lives with her mum. Like I live with my sister.' Ross grinned.

Darcie's heart contracted. 'Do you feel different to your friends?'

He folded the gum into his mouth. 'How do I know how everyone else feels?' He tried, with several movements of his head, to flick his hair out of his eyes. When this failed, he turned his forehead against the back of the settee and used it to wipe the hair back. 'Being different doesn't matter, does it?' He frowned, his chewing becoming faster, jerkier. 'You're still cool about me?'

Eyes prickling, she touched his hand. 'Absolutely. Completely. When we lost Mum and Dad I didn't want anything more than for us to make our home together. I would have fought the system like a superhero if some well-meaning social worker had wanted to put you with a foster family.'

Sweat formed a lustre on his cheeks. 'I dreamt about it the other night, the police coming,' he said. 'Fetching you. I knew it was bad when they wouldn't tell me till you came.' He wiped his forehead with his sleeve.

'It was a nightmare. No wonder you dream about it.'

'You know — ' He paused, cleared his throat. 'You know when you and Dean broke up, that was because of me, wasn't it?'

She was shaking her head even before he ended his sentence. 'I've told you a hundred times. My relationship with Dean was on its last legs and when Mum and Dad died and my universe had to revolve around us instead of him it just brought the end on.' It was a half-truth, but it wouldn't help Ross to go into the more complicated full version.

He stepped back a conversational subject. 'Anyway, having your parents around doesn't guarantee you a good deal. Casey's dad used to hit her, and her mum didn't do anything about it.' Then, before Darcie could formulate a response, he grasshoppered to another subject. 'Why did you act weird when Kelly said her brother will be at your party?'

She picked up her wine glass and took a sip, to make sure her voice wouldn't betray her. 'Did I? Jake and I have a bit of an up and down relationship. He isn't sweet and cheerful, like Kelly. Or, at least, not to me. He can be difficult.'

And he could be heartstoppingly fabulous. Exciting. He could set her on fire and shake her world like a kaleidoscope so that all she saw was colour.

Then he could act like a bastard. '*I assumed what we did meant something and that's why you said you'd tell Dean that it was over. So why haven't you?*'

Her next words hadn't been well chosen. '*I'm sorry. I found that I care too much to —* '

'*Cared too much! Caring too much for him didn't stop you having sex with me. If I'd realised you were available for hot one-night stands, I would've been all over you long before this. I suppose I just hadn't noticed your slutty side —* '

That's when she'd tipped a cup of coffee in his lap and he and his wounded pride had stalked off to take a job abroad. Gone in a week. And when her parents died, two days after he left, and he rang, '*Darcie, Kelly just told me. I'll come back and help you —* ' she'd just about had her fill of men, what with Dean dumping her as soon as he knew she'd be looking after Ross. And hadn't that been galling, when it was her being reluctant to end things with him when he was in trouble that had messed everything up with Jake!

'*It's OK, Jake. I can cope,*' she'd said.

2

Three-oh. Thirty. *Bleugh*. Why had she let herself be persuaded by Ross and Kelly that Mum and Dad would have thought a party a good way to spend a bit of the money they'd left her? With the DJ, the canapés, the room hire and a few free drinks, it was costing hundreds, and Darcie got a crawly sensation between her shoulder blades every time she thought about it. Since Kelly had dropped the Jake-bomb, anyway.

Darcie stared in the mirror at the willowy collection of hollows and ridges that was her. The hem of her misty blue party dress zigzagged between knee and thigh — it would have been well below the knee on most women. Her fair hair twirled unsatisfactorily down onto her collarbones. Perhaps she ought to get a good cut instead of just leaving it twiddling there. It had scarcely changed since senior school, when she'd spent her time waiting for boys her age to grow tall enough to ask her out.

Jake. His lanky frame, curling lip and contemptuous pewter eyes as unlike his sweet, roundy, pink, freckled, beaming sister as could be. He'd been tall enough —

She raked her hair with her fingers and thrust it up behind her head. One lock snaked loose at the front and one at her nape, which at least looked a bit sophisticated and less gauche-small-town girl. Clutching the knot of hair, she scrabbled through a drawer for a big silver clasp and secured the mass just as Ross shouted, 'Kelly's outside in the taxi.'

'Coming.' Darcie took a last look, narrowing her eyes at herself and drawing her mouth up into a sultry smile. It was her birthday; Ross had given her her favourite body lotion, the artisans from Wellbourne Workshops had made her mugs and keyrings and

15

cards with *30* on, and Kelly had taken her to see the *Dirty Dancing* stage show last week. Now she was going to her party. A party was fun. She refused to allow crawly feelings or Jake Belfast to spoil it.

★　★　★

A couple of hours later, the Anglian Room of The Bettsbrough Arms Hotel vibrated with music and the floor seemed to bounce beneath Darcie's feet. Laughing yelling faces flickered dizzyingly in the red-blue-green lights. She couldn't get to the bar without being sidetracked by one of the legion of friends she'd made in her thirty years living in the same town, from school, from Wellbourne Workshops, from just about everywhere.

At the side of the room hung a four-foot-high cardboard *30*, painted red and edged in silver foil. Ross was standing on the edge of the dance floor. She'd said he could bring three friends and he'd chosen Ben and Amy. And Casey. Ross, drinking a pint of what Darcie hoped was shandy, was stooped over listening to Casey. Amy, her back to Casey, talked animatedly to Ben.

Darcie paused beside them. 'How's the footie, Ben?' Ross and Ben had been friends since year five. Ben's parents were taking Ross on holiday with them this year; they'd be off to the Algarve in less than two weeks.

Ben, with the pale lashes and numerous freckles that went with sandy hair, smirked bashfully. 'Got Man of the Match, today. Um, Happy Birthday.'

'Happy Birthday,' echoed Amy.

'Thanks.' Darcie turned to Casey. 'Enjoying yourself?'

Casey looked up at her with her small, dark eyes, and nodded.

Obviously, Casey was disguising her enjoyment well. Darcie moved on, finally reaching the bar to order a bottle of water and a glass of wine. She was taking her first, thirsty gulps from the water, eyes closed at the pleasure of satisfying a thirst born of a hundred half-shouted conversations, when Kelly's voice came from behind. 'Here she is! Darcie, Jake's here.'

Slowly, Darcie took a last swallow. Turned.

Jake.

Simple white shirt and black jeans, corn-coloured hair gleaming under the lights; his clean-shaven jaw line was an elegant angle. But she'd prepared for this moment; had known all evening it would come. She had her smile all ready. 'Hello, Jake.'

'Happy birthday, Darcie.' He stepped forward to brush his lips across her cheek-bone. The touch was warm and soft. Tingly. 'Kel said you wouldn't mind her inviting me to your party. I told her you probably would.' His smile was mocking, probably trying to prompt her into protesting that of course he was welcome. His abrasive personality hadn't changed. And he was still hot, with his one-sided smile. That was how he'd smiled at her after —

'Kelly's invitation was 'plus one'. It doesn't make any difference to me who she brings.'

He raised an eyebrow. 'Ah. I'd forgotten that you're indiscriminate.'

Darcie tamped down hissing fury at the barb designed to be understood only by her, and managed a smile. 'You only think that you know me.'

Kelly laughed but groaned. 'Come on, you two, don't dig at each other every time you meet. Jake's driven from Garmisch-Partenkirchen in his BMW Z4.'

'But I don't think it was just for my party. Let's dance with your Auntie Chrissy, shall we, Kelly?' Auntie Chrissy ran the gallery shops at Wellbourne Workshops and Darcie had known her so well and for so long that she had pretty much forgotten Chrissy wasn't her own aunt. She slung her arm around her friend and swung away onto the dance floor, bumping shoulders and laughing. And not looking at Jake.

★ ★ ★

After midnight, the music had slowed and mellowed, and so had the atmosphere, as the lights pulsed gently. Despite feeling Jake's presence like a brooding gargoyle all evening, though he'd turned his back to the room, propping up the bar with all his old Bettsbrough mates, Darcie had thrown herself into enjoying her party, dancing and circulating — with a little drinking thrown in.

She was just draining another glass of wine when his voice made her jump. 'I'd better claim a dance before you fall over.'

She raised her eyebrows. 'I'm not even wobbly. It's you that's been at the bar all night.' Damn. Now she'd given away the fact that she'd noticed.

Jake pushed back his hair, only the hard brightness of his eyes betraying any alcohol in his system. 'Kel insisted I exhibit my good manners by dancing with the hostess and I needed a few drinks before I could face it.'

She opened her mouth to issue a stinging retort — if she could just think of one — but he'd already taken her hand and was tugging her onto the dance floor.

Rather than draw attention by yanking away from him, Darcie accepted the warmth of his hands at her waist and rested hers lightly on his shoulders. After they'd swayed together for a minute in stiff silence, she decided conversation could hardly be less comfortable. 'How's Germany?'

'Great, I loved to be near the mountains. But I've just left that job.'

Darcie glanced into his face. 'Kelly didn't tell me.'

He grimaced. 'I've only just told her, this evening. I was sacked. Woman trouble.'

Oh. She swallowed. Well, what had she expected? It had been two years since they spent the night together and when he'd tried to reach out to her in the aftermath of the terrible car crash that had stolen her parents from her, she'd shut him out. He was an exciting, incredible-looking man, ergo he would have women. He was also a brooding, arsey, contrary ratbag, ergo he would have woman trouble.

'To be honest, I got in a public swearing match with the owner's wife.' He moved his hand into the small of her back, pulling her closer to avoid a collision with another couple.

She jumped, trying to ignore the heat that shimmered through her as their bodies touched. His eyes were colour-less in the low light, like a werewolf's. 'Wow. Didn't she like you?'

He grinned, humourlessly. 'She liked me way too much. I didn't think an affair with her would be good for my career. Turns out not having an affair had the same effect.'

'Didn't you tell your boss?'

He shook his head. 'Too messy. I like him, Josef, and the end result would probably have been the same because however things worked out between them, he wouldn't have wanted me around.'

'What are you going to do?'

'Getting another job would be good. I received almost weekly headhunting offers when I was the erratic, charming, occasionally rude Englishman *direktor* of SpaGrimmlausch. But once I'd committed the cardinal sin of offending Josef's wife, I was as welcome as water at a bier fest. And, obviously, there are people going after jobs in leisure management who can produce a reference, something that's sadly lacking in my life. So I'm surfing Kelly's sofa, as Mum and Dad retired to Cornwall and bought a one-bedroomed apartment, so there's no more room there than at Kel's.'

A burst of laughter, and a couple tangoed enthusiastically by, cheek against cheek. Jake swung her out of the way again, thighs touching, hips brushing. Then he relaxed his hold and she tried hard to convince herself it didn't affect her.

After a couple of beats, his voice

dropped. 'I was sorry to hear about your parents. It must have been hideous for you and your brother.'

The familiar lump leapt to her throat. 'Thank you.'

His eyes were level with hers, even though she was six foot two in her stilettos. 'Kelly says you've been wonderful with your little brother. He seems like a nice kid — Kelly brought him over for a bit of a chat, earlier. But . . . '

'But?' she prompted.

He took a deep breath and Darcie felt his collarbones lifting through the fabric of his shirt. 'What the fuck *happened* with Dean? You decided you 'cared too much' about him to end the relationship — '

She froze. 'That wasn't all I was trying to say. It's all you *listened* to — '

'Yet Kelly says he left right after the accident.'

Thrusting both hands against his chest, Darcie propelled herself backward, treading all over some blameless couple behind. 'Yes. He dumped me. Does that make you feel better?'

'That's not what I meant!' Jake made a grab for her, but she was too quick, gone in a rustle of fabric and a flick of hair. He hissed under his breath, 'Fuck!'

And, great, now his sister was glaring ferociously at him from the encircling arms of a guy he recognised from her year at school. She hoisted both eyebrows in an unspoken, *What have you been up to?*

He shrugged. *Nothing.*

She flicked her gaze pointedly in the direction of Darcie's retreating back, and then back at him. *It looked like something.*

He shook his head slightly. *It was nothing.* He'd just made Darcie think he was being a bit of a shit. Nothing new there, then.

3

'Hey.'

'Hey, Casey.' Leaning on the lamp-post in the car park on the edge of Blossom End, Ross had watched the small figure approach whilst he pretended to fiddle with his phone. It wasn't properly dark yet, but the lamp was already on, a sulky orange in the drizzly evening. He was content to hang around like this now Casey had explained, in clipped and ashamed sentences, that the reason he couldn't call for her at her house was that it was the one you could see from the road — with the knee-high grass and the rubbish in the front garden. She'd asked him to wait out of sight of it.

He turned and fell into step beside her and reached casually for her hand. 'Haven't seen you for a couple of days, since my sister's party.'

She pushed her hands into her pocket. 'Hiding out in my room. Dad's found where we're living and he's hanging around.' She cast a furtive look behind her.

'Crap.' Ross picked up the pace, down the hill, leaving Blossom End safely behind. They stopped at the corner shop at the junction of Queen's Road and King's Road, a popular place to hang out, and bought apple-flavoured chewing gum. When Ross made to stroll on up the hill, Casey halted. 'I can't stay out long. I want to get back before Mum goes to bed, in case Dad's lurking.'

Ross tried not to sigh as his insides sank in disappointment. 'Don't you get pissed off in your room, on your own?'

Casey folded her stick of gum in three before popping it into her mouth. 'I talk to Unsad Zag.' She laughed. When she laughed it transformed her face, curved her normally sulky mouth into prettiness, lighting her eyes.

Ross grinned. 'Who's Unsad Zag?'

There was a big blocky bench beside a patch of grass near the shop, and they settled on it. Casey sectioned off a piece at the front of her hair and began to plait it. 'You just want to laugh at me,' she pouted, peeping through the hair.

'Not.' But he did laugh. 'Go on. Tell me.'

She tucked the plait behind her ear and began on another section. 'Unsad Zag is a gnome. He's my friend, and no one else can see him.'

'How do you know?'

She frowned. 'Because he's *my* Unsad Zag. He's got a blue hat and a grey curly beard. And a big nose with a fat end.' She smiled wistfully. 'When I was little, some neighbours used to have a plastic garden gnome like that, I could see him through my bedroom window. A family lived in the house. The kids always looked happy and sometimes they played with the gnome. I used to watch them, making up stories about how the gnome knew I was sad and needed him more than the happy

28

children. And, one day, I saw him in my room. ''Ullo, m'duck,' he said, 'Ent you allowed out to play?' And that was how I got Unsad Zag.'

Ross began on his second stick of green gum. He was aware that a girl of Casey's age still depending on made-up stories to comfort herself was a bad thing. 'So he became your imaginary friend?'

Casey turned on him, with tickling thin fingers digging right under his ribs to double him up. 'Unsad Zag is not imaginary! He's *invisible*!'

'Geddoff, geddoff!' Ross yelled with helpless laughter. Did he want her to get off? She was touching him. She was being playful like most of the other girls he knew, instead of quiet and troubled.

'Then say Unsad Zag's not imaginary.'

'Not.'

'Say it properly.'

'Geddoff! Unsad Zag is not imaginary.'

'He's invisible.'

'OK, he's invisible.'

Casey took her tickling fingers back, and slid a little away. She began on a third plait. 'Unsad Zag sometimes seems like the only friend I've got.'

'He's not.' Ross slid after her, his jeans scraping softly on the well-worn wood of the bench. He placed his arm gently around her shoulders. She jumped up. 'Ross, I — !'

'I was just being friendly.' He folded his arms, awkwardly.

'I just can't be . . . be like that with anybody. Because of my dad, I don't like people too close. He tried to be . . . inappropriate with me.'

Ross felt his face heat up with mortification. 'I didn't know. Sorry.' Now her standoffishness made sense. He licked suddenly dry lips. 'What . . . ?'

She looked at her watch. 'I don't like talking about it. I better go back.'

'I'll walk up the hill with you.' He got up and fell into step beside her, casting around for another subject. 'Ben's lost his phone. He had it on Saturday night, it must've fallen out of his pocket. His parents are going to go apeshit if he has to tell them.'

Casey pulled a face. 'That sucks.' They crossed the junction and began back up King's Road. 'I've got a mate who does reconditioned phones, if he's interested. iPhone, wasn't it? I'll get him a price if he wants. 'Course, it's no good if his oldies wrote the serial number down, they'll know it's a different phone. You'd better find out.'

'Fantastic,' said Ross, absently, his mind on what Casey had just told him and whether it was OK or not to let his arm brush hers as they walked. 'I'll ask.'

4

Darcie spent some of her most contented hours at work in her space at Wellbourne Workshops, on the edge of town. Owned and administered by a trust, the art deco ex-factory building was popular with the kind of visitors who liked watching lumps of clay turn into pots, or glass and lead morph miraculously into lampshades, and visiting the gallery shop.

Now, Wednesday afternoon, Darcie had gone into Kit's workshop to the kiln they shared — they never fired at the same time because of the different temperatures needed for clay and for glass, but sharing divided costs.

Darcie watched Kit slide the last of her unfired mugs delicately onto the trolley or 'car' that shuttled in and out of the kiln, careful not to squash any of the little clay noses that would become part of a variety of expressive faces painted on for glazing. The permanent clay sludge on Kit's clothes declared her a potter, just like the sugar-like glass dust that shredded what Darcie wore told of her own craft. One final check from the front of the car to make sure that all vulnerable handles were safely tucked away, a last moment adjustment to a ceramic shelf support, and Kit said, 'Ready?'

'Heave!' Darcie added her strength to Kit's and, with a groan and a squeak of wheels on rails, the car eased into the chamber. Darcie straightened up. 'Home-time coffee in my workshop before we leave?' As she had the corner unit, Darcie's was the largest space at the Wellbourne and was the unofficial coffee break stop.

Kit beamed, her glasses glinting in the late afternoon sunshine slanting through the window as she set the kiln's timer so that the pots would fire overnight. 'You get the kettle on and I'll get the others. Chrissy will be closing the shop any time now.'

The artisans all loved colourful, bubbly, round and wobbly Chrissy for the huge energy she threw into selling the craft work to the visitors, providing the artisans with the major part of their income. Since Kelly's Uncle Bobbie had decided, after thirty years, that marriage wasn't for him, Chrissy had been a bit less bubbly and a lot less organised, but that hadn't lessened anybody's love for her. The gallery shop being open seven days a week in spring and late into the summer, Mondays and Tuesdays were covered by a thin dreamy sixty-something called Fiona, perfectly nice, but not Chrissy. Darcie found herself choosing her days off to coincide with Chrissy's. Auntie Chrissy was the spirit of the place.

Back in her own workshop with the acrid smell of solder in the air, Darcie hummed as she filled the kettle and set out mugs. She loved her friends joining her in her space — Kit, Auntie Chrissy, Wendy, who made fabulous wicker-work, and Stu, a modeller who was finding commercial success with clay tiles of the façades of local landmark buildings. They each spent long hours in their own areas and it was nice to have a bit of companionship, sometimes.

Stu inhaled loudly as he strode in. 'Mm, coffee smells good, Darcie.'

Wendy was just behind him. 'I've got biccies.'

Chrissy popped through the door in time to pass the steaming mugs around whilst the others settled themselves on the stools, chairs and one old car seat that comprised the seating. 'So did you enjoy your party? My head's still aching.'

'Brilliant!' Darcie hoped that her beaming smile looked more natural and convincing than it felt.

Kit helped Wendy open the biscuits. 'Me and Dennis haven't danced so much in years.' She craned to peer through the doorway, open to let in some of the fresh May air. 'Who's this drawing up in the yard?' she said, thickly, through half a custard cream. Visitors parked in the main car park; they were supposed to leave the area in front of the workshops clear.

'It's Jake,' said Auntie Chrissy.

Darcie was already sighing. If anyone was going to break the rules it was going to be the man now levering himself from his left-hand drive BMW Z4. 'What does he want?'

Auntie Chrissy sent her a reproachful look. 'I asked him to come up and see me. Woohoo, Jake, we're in here!'

'Right. Of course.' In the shock of seeing him so unexpectedly, Darcie had momentarily forgotten that Chrissy was Jake's aunt just as much as she was Kelly's.

Jake crossed the yard with long strides, hair blowing back from his face, and jumped lightly up the steps into the workshop. Inside, he paused, his eyes taking everyone in, then settling on Darcie. 'Hi.' He eyed her warily, as if any sudden movement might cause her to shatter. She almost wished she could, without warning, like an overheated piece of glass — *BANG!* And Jake would dance back with tiny shards of Darcie stinging and burning his skin.

But as she was made of flesh and bone and not really the kind to wish bodily pain on anyone, she just said, 'Coffee?' And got up to make it whilst Auntie Chrissy made sure that Jake knew everyone and found him a seat on the old saw stool that Darcie inherited from the woodworker who'd rented this workshop before her.

Jake looked completely at ease as he chatted to everyone, taking over *her* coffee break, Darcie thought, resentfully. Her pleasure in the end-of-day ritual of hometime coffee break fizzled away like spit on a fire as Wendy, Kit and Stu smiled and chatted and generally welcomed Jake into their midst. His air of ease made Darcie's shoulders bunch and, not feeling equipped to pretend that he didn't affect her, that she didn't want him to smile and glitter at her, too, she developed a sudden strong urge to remove herself from his presence. 'I'll have to make it a quick cuppa, today,' she decided on the spur of the moment, glancing at her watch regretfully, as if she had somewhere important to go.

'OK,' said Stu, who tried never to be any trouble to anyone, gulping his drink.

Wendy looked puzzled and took another biscuit to dunk. 'But you haven't even begun your coffee, Darcie.'

Darcie flushed. 'I've only just remembered that I have to — ' She stopped, trying frantically to think of something that sounded suitably urgent.

But Auntie Chrissy came to her rescue. 'We can move up to the shop,' she suggested. 'I want a little chat with Jake, anyway. That's why I invited him up here.'

★   ★   ★

Hurrying everyone away meant that Darcie arrived home early. Ross and

Casey were camped out in the sitting room playing Wii games on the TV, feet up on the coffee table. Ross had discarded his trainers but Casey was wearing black ankle boots ornamented with several buckles.

Darcie allowed her irritation to transfer from Jake to Casey. 'Do you think you could take your boots off, Casey, if you're going to put your feet on the furniture?'

Slowly, Casey bent her legs and began to draw them towards her. Another moment and her feet were safely on the floor. But there had been a telltale squeak, and Darcie was left staring at a deep scratch in the surface of the oak table that Mum had kept polished and pristine for years. She glanced at Casey's shuttered face, waiting for the apology, prepared to be forgiving even though she felt an echo of the scratch on her heart, because she knew that Ross's friends usually meant no harm and were just not quite used to keeping control of the strange new body that went with puberty. But Casey just kept her gaze on the TV and continued to manipulate the Wii controller as a car roared along a race track on the screen.

'You've scratched the table,' Darcie pointed out, evenly, heat rising at the back of her neck at this incredible rudeness.

And Casey threw her Wii controller on the floor. 'This is such bullshit!' she yelled as she leapt to her booted feet. And, to Ross, 'See. She hates me.' Snatching up her jacket, she barged past Darcie, out into the hall and through the front door. Slam.

Shocked, Darcie looked at Ross. But he threw down his controller, too — though onto the more forgiving surface of the sofa — and began to jam his feet into his trainers. 'Did you have to?' he snapped, not looking at Darcie.

'What did *I* do?' Darcie reeled as Ross brushed past her, too.

He swung on her, as tall as Darcie, now, and already broader. 'She doesn't have a nice home and she's not used to nice things, right? This is somewhere that she felt safe, for once, and now you've gone and fucked it up.'

★   ★   ★

Ross caught up with Casey halfway down Queen's Road. 'She didn't mean anything, Case. Darcie's cool.'

'She hates me,' she sniffed, touching delicate fingertips to the black make-up around her eyes.

He halted her with a hand on her arm. For once, she didn't shake him off. 'She doesn't hate you,' he contradicted, softly, noticing the delicacy of the bones in her arm, the way her hair blew over his hand in the breeze. 'She's like loads of oldies — gets hung up on things that don't matter. She'll realise you didn't mean to scratch the table.'

'I did.' Casey started off down the hill again.

He had to run to catch up. 'What? Why?' he demanded, stupefied.

41

Head down so that her hair veiled her face, Casey's voice was tight and high. 'Because she talked to me as if I was shit.'

Ross hurried beside her, trying to process the information, to compre-hend the bitterness that would make Casey's action acceptable. Or, at least, understandable. Casey was completely silent as they waited to cross the junction.

Then, before Ross could decide on what to say, Ben appeared from the corner shop. 'Hey, Ross. Hey, Casey, did you get that phone off your mate?'

And Casey seemed to forget her tears. She reached in a pocket of her bag. 'You interested at eighty quid?'

Ben whistled and pulled an unhappy face. 'Crap. Eighty?'

Ross looked at him sympathetically. He hated to see Ben in bother like this. 'Lot of dosh, eh?'

Ben had paled beneath his freckles.

Casey closed the zip of her bag with an angry tug. 'You don't have to have it!

Just go admit to your oldies that you've lost your phone, they'll buy you a new one. Middle-class parents and all that. Maybe they've got it insured.'

Casey stared across the road while Ben fidgeted miserably.

Ross wondered whether if he put his arm round Casey casually, now, she'd let him, or whether she'd still push him off even with Ben there. She probably would, he decided. She wasn't strong enough on tact not to make him look a dork in front of mates.

'Let's see the phone,' Ben sighed. 'My parents said that if I lost this one I'd have to do work around the house till it was paid for. That'll be months.'

Slowly, Casey opened the zip again. Fishing inside, she came out with a black iPhone. 'How are you going to explain that you've changed your number?'

Ben's expression lightened. 'I thought I'd scratch this micro card so it won't work, act all disappointed and bewildered, then they'll just get me another.'

Casey nodded. 'No need to knacker up a decent one, then.' Delving back into her bag she brought out a different card. 'This is an old one of mine that doesn't work.' Deftly she made the change, then passed over the phone.

'Just like your old one,' Ross commented, to cheer Ben up.

'Except the screen isn't scratched and you can read the buttons,' Ben observed. 'My parents might notice.'

'Well, it's reconditioned,' Ross pointed out, reasonably. 'If you don't want it, just give it back. Casey's mate will understand.'

Ben turned the phone over and over. 'Even with the money left over from my birthday, I've only got seventy-five. My parents took my holiday money to change it into euros.'

'Not enough,' said Casey.

Ross saw Ben's wretched expression. He knew Ben hated being in trouble with his parents because they grounded him for, like, absolutely ever over the slightest little thing. And he was going on holiday with Ben's family in a few days, he could do without them grinding on about the lost phone all the time.

'I'll put the fiver in for you till you can pay me back,' he offered.

Ben's face lit up. 'Thanks, Ross.'

Casey put out her hand for the money.

* * *

'I want to show you something. Can you come out with me for a walk?'

Darcie jumped. She'd been half-asleep over tedious spreadsheets on her laptop and hadn't heard Ross come in. She blinked, sleepily.

Ross's chin jutted determinedly. 'Only take half an hour.'

She stretched and rubbed her eyes. 'OK. What's going on?'

'I just want to show you something.'

Curious, Darcie pulled on trainers and zipped up a green fleece to follow him through the dull evening streets, downhill, past the shop still open and shedding a pool of yellow light, across Peterborough Road at the traffic lights, and then uphill at the other side. She had no trouble working out that they were heading for the drab beige brick streets of Blossom End, where the front doors were painted one colour per court and inadequate car parks ranged around the fort-like outer walls.

Reaching the fringes of the estate, Ross led the way across a car park then halted in one of the wide entranceways into the estate.

He put his hand on Darcie's shoulder to pull her close and share his eyeline across an irregularly shaped patch of green to a point where a row of houses overlapped another. One house stood out from its neighbours like a troll at a fairy's birthday party. The front garden was a mass of thigh-high grass doing a bad job of hiding a fridge, a pram, parts of a moped and a miscellany of stuff too rusted to be identifiable. A small area of the house's outside wall was charred.

The net curtains matched only in their uniform colour of tobacco-brown, and one window was boarded over.

Ross's hair flickered against Darcie's temple, their heads close together. 'Hear that?'

She didn't have to ask what he meant. A woman's voice carried to them from within the house, muffled and indistinct but obviously scaling the heights of anger, yelling out hatred and frustration and pain.

'I wanted you to see how Casey lives,' Ross muttered, jamming his hands in his pockets.

Darcie stared at the ugly house. Neglect emanated from it like a curse.

5

Jake had quite enjoyed spending the last few days with Kelly. When Kelly had offered him her sofa it had been for a two-week visit but — with a couple of big sighs — she'd extended the invitation to cover him getting over the awful ignominy of being sacked. It was a bit of a squash and his duvet slid off the sofa whenever he turned over in his sleep, but he could put up with it. They'd talked a lot and watched all of the *Die Hard* movies in her tiny pink brick apartment on an estate that hadn't existed five years ago, a five minute walk from the older, tree-filled, red-brick and render part of town where they used to live with their parents, and Darcie still lived.

He felt a bit guilty that he'd stayed away from Bettsbrough for so long, although Kelly hadn't complained. Bettsbrough was OK, a typical market town, very

English; pretty enough with the farm fields round and the river running at the edge, stately red-brick Victorian buildings gracing the town centre.

Kelly had visited him twice in Garmisch-Partenkirchen and teased him about him having too much of a good time at SpaGrimmlausch, to make the trip home. He'd agreed that that must be it.

He hadn't told her that her best friend had laid her long artistic hands on his heart and left a scar, still waiting to heal.

There had been an otherworldliness in hooking up with Darcie. How had that giggling, annoying little kid from school grown up into such a beautiful, creative, intelligent woman that he felt himself getting tight and heavy every time he saw her? He wished he could get over the crushing knowledge that he'd allowed himself to get emotionally naked with her, just for her to stick with Dean. As if she'd tried Jake out and found Dean better. As if that night had meant so little. She wasn't to have

49

known, of course, that he'd been fighting feelings for her for a while; fighting because she'd been an item with Dean for nearly a year and he wasn't normally the guy that got involved in other people's relationships. Life was complicated enough. But that night — *that* night — there had been a spontaneous party at his old place, an attic flat overlooking North Park, in town. Kelly had been promoted at work; the local paper had run a great piece on Darcie and her cottage industry; and Jake, who had been going through a host of interviews, had been offered three jobs, all in one week. SpaGrimmlausch had been the joker, the job he'd applied for without thinking he had a chance. Would he ever have taken it if things had worked out differently with Darcie . . . ?

The party had begun as a collection of friends eating takeaway Chinese food and drinking wine. Dean, perhaps because he wasn't one of those being patted on the back for their various achievements, had gone home early on the pretext of a headache. A couple of people had declared heavy days to wake up to and had caught a lift with him. Kelly wanted to impress a guy from work she'd brought with her, and had gone off to catch a late showing French film at the local cinema. They drifted away until only he and Darcie, caught up in an absorbing discussion about the meaning of life or the rules of scrabble, or something, remained.

He'd been entranced by her expressive face, the way she leaned her head back as time passed, making her slender throat an almost irresistible destination for his mouth. And he'd suddenly said, 'Is Dean 'the one', Darcie?'

She'd paused, an arrested expression stealing over her features. Then her eyebrows lifted, as if making a discovery. 'He can't be, or I'd know, wouldn't I?'

'So you're with him because . . . ?'

The eyebrows plunged as she struggled to analyse her wine hazed feelings. 'I like him,' she decided, finally. 'I enjoy his company.' She nodded, as if agreeing with herself. Then she pulled a face. 'When he's not being high maintenance.' Finally, she shrugged. 'It's not as if there's anyone else.'

And so he'd given in to his urge, moving in slowly, gently, giving her time to repel his advances if she wanted to, and touched his lips to hers. 'There's me.'

She hadn't pushed him away. Her light brown eyes had grown larger. 'Seriously?'

He'd let his lips travel across her cheek, brushing her ear, her neck, every hair on his body rising as he explained that he had feelings for her, the kind he was finding it hard to ignore. Unexpected feelings. He'd just been watching her laughing with Kelly one day, and — literally — felt himself falling. 'It's bloody disconcerting,' he'd said.

And she'd lifted her hand and run her long fingers through his hair. 'I know. It happened for me ages ago. I just didn't think you thought of me like that.'

He hadn't asked for details. Just pulled her into his arms and, not much later, into his bed, buzzing with heat and excitement and the sensation of something amazing happening.

Until the next day. When she'd told him that she hadn't ended things with Dean. *'I found that I care too much,'* she'd begun, as if expecting him to completely understand her caprice.

Instead, his shock and hurt had poured out in a couple of venomous sentences halted only by her flying coffee cup. And that was when he'd turned and walked away, ignoring her hurt, surprised eyes. He was the injured party, right? He'd returned home and accepted the job at SpaGrimmlausch. Efficiently, he'd given up his flat, sold his car, put his furniture in store, and gone, without speaking to Darcie again, putting some ocean and a couple of countries between them.

He hadn't seen her again until last Saturday night, when she'd looked amazing in a dress that had shown a lot of her long legs, taking her defiantly over six feet in her spike heels. He'd enjoyed watching her stalk and wiggle her way through the evening like a sexy heron. Enjoyed watching her dance. Talk. Laugh. Wearing her hair up had made her look taller than ever and set him on fire. He'd longed to pull her against him and set his mouth to the soft skin of her nape.

Or haul her up toe to toe and tell her just how out of order she'd been when he'd put aside what he considered his justifiable sense of injury to ring her when Kelly had told the terrible news about her mum and dad. He'd been ready to fly home and . . . well, do something to help her. He was hazy on what, as Dean had still been in the picture. But the point was he'd been ready to abandon his brand new job for her.

And she'd dismissed him in a few snapping words.

He knew from Kelly that Darcie dated only casually since Dean. At the party, the urge to chance his arm with her again had grown to the realms of overwhelming, but it had clashed with his wounded pride, making him prickly, sarcastic and way too blunt. Guarding against the hurt blazing inside him had made what he wanted to say come out wrong. And then he'd been staring after Darcie's rigid back.

He gazed, now, at the sitting room ceiling, listening to his sister moving around upstairs. As she had to get to her job in an advertising and promotions agency in Peterborough he was careful to leave the bathroom and kitchen at her disposal during her morning routine. All he had to get up for, after all, was to face the sexy heron, bound to jab at him with her long spiky beak when she heard his news.

* * *

Jake left his car in the car park and walked up to the workshops so that Darcie had no chance to see him arrive.

55

He'd timed his visit for lunchtime, hoping that she might be more approachable if she was due to take a break.

It seemed as if his strategy was sound because she was just taking a step back to bend a critical gaze on a completed lampshade of cream and amber glass as he stepped into her workshop. She glanced up, and froze.

'Can we talk?' He glanced back out at the blue sky. 'It's a fabulous day. How about a walk to the Boatman, on the embankment?'

She looked wary. Her hair was pulled back, her sleeves rolled up; she wore faded green trainers and jeans. Somehow, she looked even hotter than she had on Saturday. 'Why?'

He smiled. 'Because I have something to tell you that you're probably going to hate, but it's going to happen anyway, so I'm looking to make it happen with as little stress as possible. And even if I'm high on your shitlist, we need to put stuff behind us.'

She watched him for several seconds without smiling back. Then, 'OK.' In a few decisive movements she grabbed up a denim jacket, a bag, and a bunch of keys, and waved him outside, where the sunshine had a lemony early summer glow, although clouds were assembling over Bettsbrough. Whilst she locked up her workshop, he gazed in the other direction, over the fields rolling away from the town, lush green and electric yellow. Birds sang loudly from nearby May trees blossoming dark pink against the sky.

There was no need to discuss the route. They both knew the footpath that would lead them to the river and where to cross to the Boatman pub. Darcie paced beside him until, as if they were still kids, they climbed a barred gate into a corn-field and followed the hedgerow until they could push through the spiky haw-thorn onto the river bank, and follow the flow to the place where a fat, black pipe emerged from one river bank and buried itself in the other.

'I've never known what the pipe carries,' Jake said, to break the silence. 'I'm not sure I want to.'

Half-circlets of spikes like the Statue of Liberty's crown guarded each end of the pipe, as if that would keep anyone off, and they stepped carefully over. In the middle of the pipe, Jake halted to watch the water. They'd perched there a hundred times when they were in their teens — probably with Kelly between them to stop them arguing. He wondered when he would officially be too old to act like a teenager. Below, the water hurried away, olive green and spangled by the sun. If either of them fell they'd be lucky to get out of the river face up. The banks were perpendicular, a faller would have to fight the current long enough to scramble out downstream in the brief moment where the bank dipped to the water before the nearby weir's powerful undertow began to drag.

Jake had survived the ride once, at sixteen, when he'd pulled it off by exerting all his strength and using every drop of the adrenalin produced by blind, bloody helpmeMum panic to get out as he battled the weir's deadly pull.

He shook the memory off, and glanced at Darcie. A Darcie devoid of animation. Staring into the gloomy water she looked as if a decent gust of wind might topple her down to meet it.

'Don't jump.' he begged flatly. 'I don't want to be a hero.'

For the first time, her eyes flickered with the ghost of a smile. 'Don't worry, you're not.'

'Look,' he said, gently. 'I can tell you're not pleased to see me. I'm sorry I was an arse on Saturday. I don't suppose you'll believe me if I say that I didn't mean to upset you. We'll put it in our past with all the other stuff, shall we? Because I'm going to be in Bettsbrough for at least two months and we'll run into one another. I don't want you to get frosty every time we meet because I don't want Kel to feel awkward.'

She shrugged. 'We can make it so we don't meet that often.'

He hesitated, then turned on the curved surface and climbed over the other row of spikes, glancing back to make sure that Darcie didn't need help. She didn't. He waited until they both had their feet firmly on the bank where the cow parsley was frothing into bloom. 'Actually, we can't. We'll meet most days, probably.' And then, when her eyebrows shot up, 'Auntie Chrissy wants to take a couple of months off to satisfy her inner hippy and travel across Europe with some friends in a minibus. I've agreed to run the gallery shop for her, while she does.'

6

Darcie stared at him for a full ten seconds. Her lips were parted in shock, her eyebrows curved into fierce little crooks. 'That's *all* I need.'

It surprised a laugh out of him. 'I didn't accept her offer just to piss you off. It gives me breathing space. She's been yearning to go on the trip but didn't want to lose the gallery shop, because she loves working there and she can't expect Fiona to work seven days a week for two months to cover. It seemed like a Godsend to her when I turned up. Her friends have been preparing for the trip for months, so all she has to do is pack up and go. She leaves on Sunday week and I'm going to do her job and housesit for her while I decide what to do next, and when she comes home she can just slot back into her old life without having lost anything.'

'It makes absolute sense for both of you.' But Darcie's air of despair was comical.

'Sorry,' he offered.

She groaned. 'You'd better buy me a sandwich and a beer, while I get over it.'

His heart gave a little hop. 'I'm glad we're going to be civilised.'

And they were civilised. They chatted about Wellbourne Workshops over sausage sandwiches, and neither of them mentioned hot sex or regrets. 'My plan is to ask each of the artisans to supply a few more affordable products in their ranges, to get visitors in a buying frame of mind. And, before you ask, Chrissy is on board with it,' he told her. And he didn't ask if she was still in touch with Dean, or still thought of him.

'That should work,' she agreed, thoughtfully. 'I could do some less complicated lampshades, and some small stuff like coasters, photograph frames and light catchers.'

'Sounds great.' He didn't drag her

across the table so that he could kiss her so hard that she'd never think of Dean again.

So it all went very well.

Until, walking back to Wellbourne, she lapsed into frowning silence.

'Have I done something?' he asked, after several minutes. 'We seem to be back in frost territory.'

She hunched her shoulders. 'Why do men always think it's about them?' Then she took a deep breath. 'Sorry. That was uncalled for. What I mean is that I'm bothered about something that happened last night, something unconnected to you.'

'Ah. So, in the interests of fostering good relationships between us, is it something you need help with?'

She shot him a look. 'Too much niceness from you is unnerving. All the time I've known you you've been acerbic, sarcastic, abrasive and blunt. I'm not sure I can cope with you being helpful.'

They climbed back over the gate and regained the footpath, birds fluttering up from the hedgerows at their approach.

'What I'm not is stupid enough to fall for your transparent attempt to goad me into an argument, which would conveniently distract me from finding out what's getting you down and probably make me say something objectionable so that you'd have every reason to keep me at a distance.'

She gave a thoughtful lift of her eyebrows. But she didn't confide. Until they were back at the workshops and she was fishing for her key, then, 'It's Ross,' she admitted. 'He's got a thing for this girl, Casey. I don't like her and I've let it show. Last night he showed me where she lives — it's horrible, Jake. A real hellhole. So now I feel guilty and Ross has turned grouchy. He's going away on holiday with his friend, Ben, on Thursday. It'll kill me if we part on bad terms. I don't really know what to do.'

★ ★ ★

'Darcie, you lost your parents and you lost Dean. You've had a horrible time. The responsibility of turning into a mother for a teenage brother would get to almost anybody. It's huge.'

A lump like a stone jumped into Darcie's throat and suddenly she couldn't speak. She just stood there, until Jake took her key, unlocked the workshop and sat her down on a stool beside her workbench while he got busy with the kettle and instant coffee.

'You've done a great job with Ross,' he said, bringing her a steaming mug and the packet of sugar with a spoon sticking out.

She tried to say, 'Thank you,' but her mouth squared itself off in a brief silent sob and she slammed a hand over it, horrified.

Jake dumped the coffee and pulled her up off the stool and into his arms. 'It's OK,' he murmured. 'It's OK to cry, Darcie.'

But she was able to beat back the tears. She just rested her forehead on

Jake's shoulder, taking a moment's comfort from the pulse of his body. One of his hands was firm in the small of her back, the other stroking her shoulder blade. She let herself sink against the heat of his chest. Solid.

She heard his breathing quicken. There was no mistaking his sudden tension. Gently, she disengaged herself, smiled weakly and picked up her coffee. 'Thanks.'

7

'They're calling our flight now. I thought I'd just call to say 'bye.'

'Yeah, 'bye. We said it last night, anyway.'

'I know we did.' Ross felt a hollow inside him at the despondency in Casey's voice. 'Will you be OK?'

'Have to be.'

'What's going on with your dad?'

Casey laughed bitterly. 'He's hanging around. Scummy bastard.'

Ross raised his voice over the droning of the PA system. 'I'll text you.'

'Yeah, you said. I won't be able to text you back unless I can get some credit. Anyway, have a great time in the sunshine in that cool villa. Have a happy holiday.'

Ross felt wracked with guilt that he was going to a Spanish villa on holiday. Not a small, grubby house in a dodgy area with bits of old pram in the front garden waist-high with weeds, stalked by a mad bastard of a father.

It sucked.

And he had a nice home to go back to . . .

Darcie made it possible for him to live in that home. The social services would have put him with foster parents, without Darcie, no matter that half the house had been left to him. His conscience pricked him. He hadn't hugged her goodbye. He thumbed a quick text to Darcie. *C U when I get back.*

In seconds, he got a big smiley face in return. *Have a great time! xxx*

★   ★   ★

At her workbench, Darcie worked on sketches of the new shades for the affordable range and tried not to look at the clock and wonder whether Ross was actually up in the air, yet. He was fifteen-years-old and with a family she knew and trusted. There was no way she should be worrying about him, especially once he'd texted her a more-or-less friendly message, like a little piece of cyber forgiveness to warm her heart.

She tried to settle to her task. The new shades would be less intricate than her more expensive individual pieces, quicker in production and suitable for making in batches. Heavy on style and proportion but light on complexity.

Absorption took over and soon she was drawing templates on squared paper with a sharp pencil. Eight panels to form a simple, scalloped shade, each panel consisting of the same pattern of three triangles and a semi-circle. She'd make up a jig to contain each panel as it was assembled, in the interests of symmetry and ease. She'd need fresh stocks of brass caps to solder over the top opening of lampshades, spiders for added strength or where a cap wasn't used, copper foil, copper wire, solder and flux.

Her workshop door stood open to let

in the breeze. And suddenly Jake was framed in the doorway. 'I'm working on the more affordable pieces you want,' she said, conversationally, as if she'd quite expected him, as if their relationship didn't have more loops in it than a roller coaster track.

'You don't waste any time.'

She gestured towards one of her Tiffany-style lampshades under construction at the end of the bench, myriad pieces of glass rosettes in glowing shades of blue and red. 'The new stuff is going to be a cinch, in comparison to something like that, which takes hours and hours of work.'

Carefully, he ran his fingertips over the smooth glass and raised lead work. 'It's beautiful.'

She gave him a quick smile. 'Every one of those pieces is an individual design, each tiny piece of glass cut to shape to make up like a 3-D jigsaw. The new stuff will still be pretty, but more basic. And I've already done a couple of coasters for you to look at. They're so quick they seem like cheating.' She pulled out a small cardboard box from under the bench, passing him a clear glass coaster with a silver swirl motif showing through from the bottom, little silicone blisters under each corner to protect delicate surfaces.

He ran his fingers over it. 'Certainly a poor relation compared to your individual pieces, but decorative and functional. It will really help the shop to have budget lines, if it's not too much of an affront to your artistic soul to turn them out.'

'My artistic soul is more affronted by my bank account being empty.'

But he'd drifted off to browse the shelves where she had completed work stored. He lifted a leaf-shaped bowl, its stalk sticking out from its rounded end like a robin's tail, and held it up to the light. The glass was almost clear at the base of the bowl, filtering to a watery green at the rim.

'Those usually sell OK.' She joined him at the shelves and lifted down a larger, oval dish, pale pink as if blushed by a winter dawn. 'These are ready for when the shop needs more stock.'

'How do you make them?'

'It's called slumping. You need a mould — I can get them made by Kit, or make them myself using her stuff — and the glass has to be fired hot enough to sag into it.'

His eyes smiled. 'You make it sound so simple.'

'It's a lot easier than the leadwork, but nowhere near as satisfying.' She replaced the bowl and moved away, wanting to put distance between her and his disturbing heat. 'You haven't taken over from Auntie Chrissy already, have you? I saw her this morning.'

He propped himself against the workbench, steering carefully clear of the area around the intricate rosette lampshade. 'No, I'm just getting the feel of the place and helping her with a stocktake.' He changed the subject abruptly. 'I was talking to Kelly and she says you should come round to hers tonight. She knows that Ross has gone on holiday and she thinks you need company and comfort food.'

She picked up her pencil and frowned down at the design she'd been working on. 'Will you be there, too?'

'Is that a problem?' His voice was neutral.

She shook her head. 'Just wondering whether to bring one bottle of wine, or two.'

'Kelly says I'm to tell you not to bring anything. She has something particular planned.'

★   ★   ★

Darcie arrived at Kelly's flat when the light was just turning to the steely blue of twilight. Kelly let her in with a cheery, 'You're just in time. I'm about to put supper on the plate.'

Darcie followed her into the kitchen, glancing around her. There were no cooking smells or signs of preparation. Gravely, Kelly selected two packets from a cupboard. 'Cornflakes or Honey Nut Cheerios?' On the table stood a bottle of Bailey's.

'Kelly, we used to do that when we were sixteen!' Darcie protested, laughing.

Kelly made her expression affronted, though her eyes shone with fun. 'And your point is?'

Jake strolled into the room, hands in pockets. 'I've been trying to remind her how drunk we got, but she's on a nostalgia trip. She thinks it'll cheer you up.'

Kelly began pouring Cornflakes into bowls. 'Don't you remember that party? I ate three bowls and was sick afterwards.'

'Me, too.' Darcie winced.

Jake snorted. 'At least you got home first. Kelly was ill in someone's front garden. We had to run away. Life's all bad behaviour and happy days when you're sixteen.'

As Kelly opened the Bailey's Irish Cream, Darcie said, wistfully, 'I bet it'll be horrible, we're not kids any more.' But she'd received another text from Ross to tell her of his safe arrival, on the walk from her house, and she was ready for her tension to dissolve. Stupid fun did seem kind of appealing. 'OK, Cornflakes.'

'Cornflakes!' Kelly poured the thick, pale liqueur over the cereal with an air of satisfaction.

Shrugging, Jake took a seat at the table in front of one of the bowls and picked up a spoon. 'Cornflakes for me, too. *Guten appetit* and cheers.'

Darcie sat down to the rolling-back-the-years supper. 'Cheers.' She took a spoon and a deep breath. The corn-flakes were crisp and the Bailey's cold and thick, smooth on her tongue but stinging the back of her throat. 'Urgghh,' she spluttered. But, after the first couple of flinching spoonfuls, the combination didn't seem too bad, even if her eyes did smart. She choked only once, and Kelly patted her considerately on the back.

Jake crunched and swallowed. 'I

wonder how it'd be with Weetabix? Maybe we could sell the idea to one of the cereal giants.'

Darcie got up to fill three large glasses with nice, cold water. 'Wow, it hasn't lost any of its potency. I feel my eyes sliding around like marbles on a tin lid already.'

Kelly took some water. 'It's because you chug it straight down, I think. But we've two more bowls to go, yet.'

'I'm not eating two more! It's lethal.'

'Don't be such a lightweight. We're reliving our youth, remember?'

'Including the being sick bit?'

Jake shook more Cornflakes out of the packet. 'No, skipping that is today's challenge.'

They spooned and chewed, grimaced and laughed. The mixture was sweetly cloying and Darcie was glad she hadn't chosen Honey Nut Cheerios. 'Don't give me any more after this, 'cos I won't drink it. Eat it. Whatever.' The words were disobedient on her tongue.

Kelly had pushed her second bowl

away. 'I think I'd better stop, or I'll fail the challenge. Maybe my sweet tooth has gone.'

Jake stirred his Cornflakes and Bailey's together and carried on eating. 'It must be nearly time to go lie on the grass and study the universe.'

Darcie's head was buzzing; she rubbed it with the flat of her hand. 'We're not doing the watching the stars thing, too?'

'The stars are there, just like they used to be.' He smiled at her. One corner of his mouth lifted more than the other.

Darcie liked Jake's smile — a hint of laughter, a flash of mischief, a gleam of what might come next. Damn, she was looking at his mouth. She looked away. 'That drink's gone straight to my legs.' Her spoon clattered into the dish. 'And my hands.'

'Shoes off, then, let's see how the grass feels on bare feet tonight.'

'Not me.' Kelly pushed herself off the chair and tottered through the archway to the sofa in the lounge area. 'It's not summerish enough.' She flopped into a corner of the sofa and scrabbled inelegantly for the TV remote.

'Wimp.' Jake took Darcie's arm and she found herself gliding beside him down two flights of stairs and out of the rear entrance of the flats to the pocket-sized communal garden. Before she had time to get her fuzzy head around whether it was a good idea, she found herself alone with him in the darkness.

★ ★ ★

The dewy garden was heavy with evening scents. The stars were already pricking the darkness. They pulled off their shoes, letting cool grass thread between their toes. He watched her slim, high-arched, pink-nailed bare feet and thought about buying her toe rings and anklets to decorate her elegant feet.

'Here.' Jake dropped down more suddenly than he'd intended to, but it did have the effect of pulling Darcie almost on top of him. Their shoulders pressed as they lay down on the moist lawn, and she didn't move away. They gazed up at the spangled navy sky.

Darcie pointed. 'Orion's Belt. The only constellation I know.'

He gazed at the three stars spaced perfectly in a row. They seemed uncomfortably bright and difficult to focus on.

'The lawn's beginning to move,' she complained, 'as if we're on a giant roundabout.' Her voice was breathy and near. He could smell her shampoo.

'We are. It's called a planet. Hold my hand, it'll kid your brain that you're being held still.'

She took the proffered hand, giggling. 'That's ridiculous.'

Her hand felt fine and delicate in his. 'It's perfect common sense. I always sleep with one foot on the floor when I'm drunk, don't you? It keeps the bed still.' He was pretty sure that his own spinning sensation had more to do with Darcie than with the Bailey's.

'I've never thought of it. I'll try it tonight.'

'You're not really drunk and you'll be sober by the time you get to bed. You're just buzzing with drinking so quickly.'

'*Brr.*' She shivered. 'Think your sister was right. It's not warm enough for this.'

He slid an arm around her and pulled her close. 'Share body heat.' She was warm and soft.

'You're nuts, wanting to lie outdoors in the dark.' Nevertheless, she allowed their bodies to press together, side-against-side.

'It's what you like most about me.' His voice had dropped several notes and could be described as relaxed. Hers was dipping into the realms of slurred.

She shifted slightly to accommodate her slender frame against the lumpy grass, and him. 'I'm not sure I like anything about you.'

''Course you do. I bought the Bailey's.'

She gave a breathy little giggle, wriggling again, kicking his pulse up at least ten points. 'I'm too thin to lie on the ground. I need upholstery.'

80

'You're not thin, you're slender. Willowy.' He thought of the angles of her cheekbones and the sexy little scoops around her collar bones.

'You used to tell me I was like a draining board and two satsumas.'

'At sixteen, I had no real idea of what words would tumble out when my lips parted. I'm better able to express appreciation, these days.' He turned to watch her profile. 'You're built like a gymnast — a stretch version. If you'd ever come to the spa you would have had everyone sighing in envy.'

Her eyes closed and she put on a languid, demanding voice. 'I'd need the full pamper treatment, of course.'

'Massage for Madam, perhaps?'

'Mmm, massage sounds *wonderful* . . . ' She opened her eyes and her mouth curled as if to laugh as she turned towards him. But when her eyes met his the laughter faded, became something else. He couldn't look away. His breathing first skidded to a halt, then set off at a gallop.

In slow motion, he dipped his head to hers. And kissed her. Gently. The softness of her mouth moved voluptuously under his, his tongue parting her lips. He shifted to let his body melt and reform to exactly fit against her. Who would've thought that a draining board and two satsumas would feel so fantastic? The sensation of the world spinning returned. So, wow, the Earth really could move.

He gave a grunt of satisfaction in his throat, sliding his hand up her ribs, skimming her shoulder blade, finding the nape of her neck as he took possession of her mouth in a kiss he felt right down in his insteps. Bare insteps that were being brushed by her dew-damp toes.

For several long, delicious moments she let it continue, letting him indulge in the unforgotten sensation of pressing together and communicating through throbbing carnal kisses.

'Darcie? *Darcie!* Are you here? Where are you?'

The kissing slowed. Stopped. In the darkness, their racing breath mingled for a last moment. Jake didn't resist as she broke away to rejoin the real world. In fact, he felt strangely weakened, like Superman getting too close to Kryptonite. But he cursed his sister, who was picking her way towards them, huddled into a coat that looked as if she'd borrowed it from Scott of the Antarctic.

Darcie's voice sounded oddly shrill. 'Kelly? We're over here.'

Kelly wobbled towards them. 'It's boring indoors on my own. I decided to come and see whether you guys are having more fun.'

8

Carefully, Darcie began to edge a piece of craquel glass — amber, a favourite of hers — with copper foil. She picked up a wooden dowel, shiny with use, and began to burnish the foil onto the glass.

She worked on in silence, applying the copper foil, burnishing, returning the piece to the jig. She concentrated on getting the fold of foil on a corner just right. Sliding on gloves, she rubbed over the glass with flux to remove any deposits preparatory to doing the initial tack-solder of the last panel of one of the new 'affordable' lampshades. She had yet to tin and bead solder the panels together, fix on the 'spider' which would take the collar of the bulb, and copper wire the lower profile for strength.

She picked up the soldering iron and wiped the point on a damp sponge, breathing in the familiar acrid smell of the iron heating up.

Her head ached slightly but she was relieved not to be hungover. Jake had been right. The Bailey's hit had been quick and hard, and had worn off by the time she'd made home.

Then, suddenly, he was there. Because it was a nice day she'd left the door open, and he'd walked softly up to watch her work. Echoes of last night tingled up her spine. In fact she'd been tingling pretty much all morning. Her hands might have been busy with cutting and grinding glass but her memories of last night had been unruly, encouraging the tingles to zip about pretty much unsupervised. But they'd been pursued by the sneaky snaky realisation that the attraction between them not being extinguished by a two-year-old unresolved misunderstanding didn't meant that the misunderstanding didn't need resolving.

Yet, if Kelly hadn't come out last night, the heat that had flared between them . . .

No. She shook herself. They would hardly have made love on a patch of grass overlooked by the rear windows of about twenty-four flats. They would have had to find somewhere — her house — and ... She would have straightened things out between them before letting the heat consume her. Wouldn't she?

Anyway, Kelly *had* come out.

She and Jake had pulled apart.

He shut the door softly behind him. 'I don't suppose I can just cut through everything else, and kiss you again?'

The tingles exploded.

Carefully, she put down her soldering iron and squared her shoulders. Calmly, she met his gaze. Hungry. Intent. Lighting a fire low in her abdomen. 'We need to talk, first.'

The heat began to fade. He sighed, folding his arms. 'We seem to communicate so well without words. That's not enough?'

She smiled faintly. 'Not for me. Stuff happened. I can't put it behind me without dealing with it.'

His jaw flexed. 'I don't see that it will help us to rake up that we once spent a hot night in bed together and you said you'd end things with Dean. Then you thought better of it.'

Anger flushed through her. 'Doesn't that depend on what I have to say?'

His voice was gentle, but final. 'I just don't see the point in stirring all the bad stuff up again, Darcie.'

A cold lump slid into her stomach. Picking her soldering iron up again she smiled, tightly. 'No. There's obviously no point. You're right. You're always right, aren't you?' Distantly, she realised that her hand was trembling, so she set the soldering iron back in its rest because trembly soldering wouldn't sell well. 'No more kisses, OK? Again — no point.'

He looked thrown by her vehemence. Belatedly, questions filled his eyes. But she jumped up, almost knocking her stool over, connected up the industrial vacuum cleaner with jerky movements and flicked it into roaring life, fixing her gaze to the nozzle that sucked up the glass debris glittering on the bench, so that he couldn't read any answers in hers. 'No point talking to people who don't listen,' she muttered.

But he must have read her lips. 'OK, let's talk,' he said, raising his voice over the angry noise of the vacuum.

'No point,' she repeated.

★　★　★

Darcie couldn't avoid Jake during the following week. Auntie Chrissy had little attention to spare for the gallery shop, so excited was she about her trip. She and 'the girls', as she called her fellow travellers, planned to set their camper van wheels spinning towards the Eurotunnel early on the next Sunday morning. Each afternoon she popped up in Darcie's workshop, saying, 'We're having coffee, aren't we? I'm dying to tell you about . . . ' And brought Jake with her.

Perfectly understandable, Darcie told herself. He was not only working alongside Chrissy as she passed over responsibilities to him, but he'd known Darcie most of his life, so why would Chrissy even check if Darcie minded?

He could have made excuses and stayed away, Darcie thought, darkly. But he never did.

And if Jake felt awkward around Darcie, he hid it well. His grey eyes were veiled when they rested on her. He was polite, but he talked to Kit, Stu and Wendy more than he talked to her, learning the particular attractions of models, wicker or pottery, and how he was going to sell them, making them smile and laugh and open up to him. He'd always been able to switch on the charm. Darcie remembered her mum saying, 'That boy will get by on his personality. He can talk to anybody.' Perhaps dealing with guests who could have bought the spa dozens of times over had polished the skill.

He joined the chorus thanking her

for the coffee when the break was over, but then he usually left. Even when he lingered one day to study the stock she had building, making her wonder if it was an excuse to hang on as the others went to close up for the day, he just said, 'You're outselling everybody, your affordable stuff is walking off the shelves.' And strolled out, hands in pockets.

Ross returned late on Wednesday, banging the doors of Ben's parents' car, shouting his thanks, bursting into the house with his case and backpack, a wind-up bull under his arm. He paused when he saw Darcie, uncertainty flickering over his face. He was tanned, his jaw line emphasised by boyish stubble and Darcie experienced a funny folding of the stomach, knowing that he was growing up and away from her and Jake's words floated through her mind: *You've had a horrible time. Turning into a mother for a teenage brother would get to almost anybody. It's huge.* OK, it was a huge responsibility — just not horrible. Since they'd lost their parents, she was much more than a big sister. She was all Ross had until he was old enough for independence.

His wellbeing had to be her main concern. She'd turned on her 'mothering', for Ross and if she had no idea how she was going to turn it off again, well she'd push that worry aside for now. Her priority was to banish any lingering suspicion and resentment, not allow it to eat away at the closeness that had, till now, allowed her to watch over Ross without turning into a hated authority figure.

She'd spent the evening, whilst she waited, not-watching TV and failing to stop Jake Belfast's face from floating into her mind. But Ross barging in grabbed all of her attention. She leaped up and threw her arms around him. 'You look great! Did you love it? Were Ben's parents OK?'

After only the smallest of hesitations, he hugged her back, his cheek rough against hers. Her heart expanded with relief as he grinned and returned to the real Ross, the pre-outburst Ross, pouring out the story of his holiday in the sun, how Ben's 'oldies' had been difficult to convince that fifteen was almost adult, the beach had been awesome and the under-18 clubs wicked.

Darcie took the bull and the backpack to carry up to his room, letting his words flood over her, and her heart lifted for the sheer joy of having him back in the house, which had seemed so empty without him.

OK, so things weren't going to work out with Jake. No change there, then. They hadn't worked out before. She was used to it. He was so intransigent, so black-and-white . . . she couldn't see things working out in the future, either.

Ross: *he* was her future. At least short term.

When he paused for breath, she put in, 'Has Casey been OK while you've been away?' to ensure that Casey didn't become a taboo subject between them.

Frowning, Ross pulled out his phone and flicked at the screen. 'I don't know. I haven't heard from her.'

9

Jake looked around the Westbourne Gallery Shop. The stands held displays calculated to entice visitors to pour money into the till and take home as much as they could carry.

But rain, pounding against the windows, made an influx of morning visitors unlikely. It was Sunday, usually the busiest day, and Chrissy had already phoned him, excited and squeaky at being carried off in a camper van. After work, he'd move his stuff into her house in Pebble Lane, which would, at least, provide him with a bed he could spread out in and get him out of his sister's hair. But he wondered, bitterly, how come Chrissy was the one heading for the open road whilst he was stuck in a shop. He sighed.

A shop was so not him. Soooo not.

He thought of the spa in the forest

where the moneyed people went to play. His job had let him be the guy who made the spa experience whatever the guests wanted it to be without ever doing any particularly onerous work himself. SpaGrimmlausch's budget had allowed for a small army of staff for him to direct around the plush serenity of what had once been a *burg*, a gothic mini-castle, scented with fragrant oils and lotions indoors, pine trees out, where the weather didn't matter because, once inside the tall grey walls, the guests could ignore it.

Not like here, where he was staring through the window of a shop without customers across a rainswept yard to where Darcie would be bending her head over her work.

He thought of her face after he'd kissed her beneath the stars, eyes a sultry window to her soul.

But he'd seen those big Bambi-eyes two years ago, when she'd rocked on top of him in his bed, luminous with excitement as he held her gaze and moved inside her, feeling as if his heart was slowly being fucked from his body.

It had only taken one dance with her for him to realise that the feelings had never gone away.

He hunted around the shop for distraction, wishing he hadn't spent so much of last week helping Chrissy sorting and stocktaking, so that the work was still there to do. He headed for the stock room and tidied some cardboard boxes. Turned on the computer in the alcove between the stock room and the shop that served as an office. Checked his email. Paid a couple of bills.

Nearly lunchtime. A handful of customers, tiring of waiting for the rain to let up and venturing out to do something with their Sunday. One bought a set of Darcie's coasters. Another lull.

Four more customers, women in their fifties, laughing at Kit's expression mugs, examining Wendy's wickerwork, spotting buildings they knew in Stu's local landmark tiles. Pausing, awed, in front of the most fabulous of Darcie's lampshades, cream lotus flowers and pale blue sky. 'Better not pick it up,' murmured one. 'It's too expensive to drop. It's like a rainbow in glass, isn't it?' She turned to Jake. 'These shades aren't made here, are they?'

'Of course,' he assured her, airily. 'You can meet the creator, if you like. She's working this morning and she never minds chatting to visitors. I'll lock the shop for two seconds and take you over.'

And as he led them through the downpour like a duck with ducklings, he wondered how long it would be before he admitted to himself that he'd taken this job because of all the opportunities to see Darcie.

★ ★ ★

Darcie looked up as her door flew back and strangers surged in, laughing, shaking back their hoods, flicking rain from their hair. Automatically, she smiled a greeting. All of the artisans made the visitors, their livelihoods, welcome.

'It's pouring down!'

'We've just been admiring — '

'This gentleman said you wouldn't mind — '

A taller figure filled the doorway behind them. Jake. Raindrops glistened on his cheekbones and spotted his shirt darkly. 'These ladies would like to meet you, Darcie. They like your work.' He spoke easily, warmly, as if there had never been an instant's tension between them.

Taking her cue, she pushed forward the half-built lampshade in front of her. 'Would you like to see what I'm working on? I'll explain the technique, if you'd like that. It's a commission and the client wants what he calls 'church window colours' of ruby, leaf green and royal blue, as his house is a converted chapel in a nearby village.'

The women crowded around the

bench. 'If you don't mind?'

'That would be — '

'Your work's so — !'

Darcie began her spiel. 'Stained glass is created when metallic salts are added at the time of manufacture. As well as in churches, it's used in houses and public buildings. It was particularly popular in art deco buildings, and you can find several original examples around the Wellbourne Workshops.'

But, as they huddled closer, the door flew open again and Ross and Ben fell in, dripping rain from their sports bags. 'We're drenched,' began Ross. Then, seeing Darcie wasn't alone. 'Oops. Sorry.' And, then, to Jake, 'Hey. Kelly's brother, right?'

Jake nodded. 'Right. Hey.'

Darcie smiled her apologies at the visitors. 'Ross, whatever made you come out in this weather?'

'You!' Ross squelched across the wooden floor. 'You said you'd leave me the £40 I need for the rugby trip. I've got to pay it at two o'clock training today. Ben paid his before we went on holiday.'

Ben nodded, scrunching his shoulders against drips sliding from his hair. 'Deadline today.'

'Rats! I forgot all about it. I meant to go to the ATM last night and leave you the money, this morning.' Darcie cast a hunted glance at her watch and an apologetic one at the visitors. 'I'm so sorry, but I'll have to make a quick dash to the ATM — '

'It's OK,' interrupted Jake, 'it's pointless shutting up your workshop, Darcie. My wallet's in my jacket, at the shop. Come with me, Ross. Your sister can pay me back when she's replenished her cash supply.'

'Cool,' said Ross, turning instantly to follow the source of money out of the workshop. 'Bye, Darcie.'

'Oh, but — !' Darcie began. But then she was staring at the closing door and the ladies were still there looking expectantly at her, so she swallowed her frustration and managed a smile as she

100

began to talk about cutting and grinding glass.

But, damn it to hell. She didn't want to be beholden to Jake Belfast.

10

Bemused, Ross surveyed the bounty spread out on the kitchen table — mobile phones, handheld games consoles and MP3 players. He looked levelly at Casey. 'They're not nicked, are they?' Casey had been waiting like a parcel on the doorstep when he'd arrived home after rugby practice. He was glad he'd showered off the mud and sweat in the clubhouse.

She opened her eyes very wide and tossed back her black hair. 'You know that I've got a mate who reconditions stuff. Kids sell him their phone so they can get a newer one. Or buy a new iPod off him if they've lost theirs and daren't tell their mums, like Ben. My mate's got loads of stuff at the moment and wants to shift it.'

Ross checked out one or two of the phones, they seemed pretty up-to-date for trade-ins. 'So what's the deal?'

'Here's a price list. You get twenty per cent of everything you sell. If you discount something, more fool you, he still gets eighty per cent of the list price, any discrepancy comes out of your cut.'

Ross's palms were uncomfortably clammy as he picked up a Nintendo DS and checked that it worked. 'And you're sure they're not nicked?'

She flung her arms up. 'C'mon Ross, I thought you were up for this. I told him how you've got so many friends you'd be sure to shift some stuff.'

He picked up an iPhone. 'What's his name, your friend?'

'It's no one you know.' She pulled a lock of hair forward to plait it.

Ross put the phone back and folded his arms. 'If he hasn't got a name, I'm not selling his stuff. It's dodgy.'

Casey sighed. Ross began to shove the stuff back into her bag. She stopped him with a hand on his arm. 'Ross, don't get heavy.' The hand squeezed persuasively. 'Colin Jones, OK? His stuff's not nicked, but he doesn't pay tax, that's why he doesn't want his name mentioned.'

His skin tingling where she touched him, Ross covered her hand with his. 'Why are you so keen to help him?'

Casually, she extricated herself. 'He pays me a fee for everything you sell. Money to put credit on my phone and buy stuff I need when my mum's skint, OK? Now stop being such a dork.'

★　★　★

If Ross had to go to school, Rowland Community College was OK. It had a good computer suite and sports facilities, and there were no more despotic teachers or thuggish kids than at any other school. And Casey went there, though he didn't normally see much of her in school. She was one of the invisible sixth formers who found their own areas to lurk in.

Ross swung in through the students' entrance of the humanities block with his backpack dangling negligently from one shoulder, and made for level 2, where his locker stood against a wall.

His bag was ridiculously heavy. He stashed his afternoon books in the locker.

'Hey, Ross.'

He turned, with a grin. 'Hey, Amy! How you doing? Hardly see you these days.'

What he meant was it was nice that she had stopped ignoring him. He'd been sorry that Amy had taken his getting close to Casey as a sign that she'd been dumped. When he'd closed his locker, they fell in step along the corridor, he heading for Mr Cooper's registration group, her for Mr Sharpe's.

Amy's fair hair was twisted into a rope over one shoulder, shedding on her navy school sweatshirt. 'I never see you, Killengrey, doesn't that girlfriend of yours ever let you off the lead?'

He laughed. 'Casey's not my girl-friend.'

Amy sniffed. 'All the more reason to

get a life away from her.'

'She's my friend.'

They stopped by rooms 56 and 57 and leaned on the radiators. None of the cool kids went into registration until the last possible minute. 'You used to have loads of those, before you took up with Casey McClare.'

He stared at her. 'I have got loads.'

She pushed the rope of hair back. 'So why do I keep seeing Ben and Jonny out without you?'

It was an uncomfortable thought; maybe he ought to make a bit more effort, maybe on the evenings when he didn't see Casey.

Later, Ross made sure to walk out of school with Ben and invite him round that evening.

Ben said. 'I've already arranged to go out with Jonny and Amy.'

'I might come.'

Ben shrugged. 'If you like.'

They were almost at the main road where their routes diverged. 'Phone still going all right? Only I've got some of those that Casey's mate reconditions, if you're interested.'

Ben flushed. 'I'm OK, thanks.' He turned and walked quickly towards his home without telling Ross where to meet up that evening. He shrugged, and got his phone out to text Casey. He'd sold an iPod, today.

★　★　★

She was waiting on the usual bench near the junction of Queen's Road and King's Road. 'Here you are,' he said as soon as he plumped down beside her. 'Fifty quid.'

Casey beamed. 'Give me forty, then, I'll pass it on to . . . Colin.'

Instead, he handed over the whole fifty. 'You have my share.'

She beamed even more widely 'Let's go get chips. I'm starving.'

Outside the chip shop, they saw Ben, Jonny and Amy. As he and Casey queued, Ross saw through the window that Jonny and Amy stood dead close together. Ben looked a bit lost, standing alone and messing with his phone. Ross's stomach tightened. Ben had been his best mate forever.

'We could hang out here,' he said as Casey led the way out of the chip shop, stabbing hungrily at her chips with a wooden fork.

Turning on her heel, Casey simply walked away. Ross hesitated, then followed, feeling slightly stupid. 'What's up?'

She shrugged. 'Nothing. I just saw the time. I'm going.' But then she stopped, staring at a bedraggled figure that had suddenly appeared, his leather jacket ripped and a can of lager in his grubby hand, beard and hair straggly and unwashed.

Ross stepped up beside Casey, protectively. 'It's OK. Just some old wino. Wait till he's gone.'

The man staggered to a halt. He wasn't a big guy; smaller than Ross but still bigger than Casey. 'Gimme some change. I need a cuppa tea.'

'Got none,' Ross said, briefly.

'Anything will do.' The man smiled winningly at Casey, displaying more gaps than teeth. 'You must have somethin'.'

'Piss off!' Casey snapped.

Then suddenly the man was shouting, right in Casey's face, close enough that Ross could see the seams of dirt engrained in his skin. 'Gimme some change! I need a cuppa tea!'

He thrust out his hands and Ross didn't wait to see where the wino intended them to land. He dropped his cone of chips and planted his hands on the man's skinny shoulders under his slimy old jacket, and shoved. The man staggered and fell over. Slowly, in the horrified silence, he rolled back to his feet, still clutching his can of lager, hardly seeming to have spilled a drop. As if nothing had happened, he weaved away along the pavement, around the corner and out of sight.

Casey hadn't moved.

'You OK?' Ross asked, awkwardly, sliding an arm around her shoulders.

His touch seemed to bring her back

to life, and she shook it off. 'That was my dad. Leave me alone.'

Frozen, Ross watched her stump away, head down and hair flying in the breeze. Then, aware of the others, their expressions registering surprise and sympathy, glanced down at his scattered chips, lying on the pavement in a cloud of steam and vinegar.

Ben, Amy and Jonny looked on, unspeaking. 'See you later,' Ross managed and as he set off up the hill towards Eaton Road the comments they didn't make about Casey's behaviour followed him home like sly dogs.

Ten minutes later, he shoved open the door into the house.

'Hi, Ross,' Darcie called.

He threw a glance into the sitting room as he passed. Darcie was lounging across one of the chairs, feet dangling, Kelly curled up in the other, both looking away from the TV with ready smiles.

'Hey,' he said, briefly, not pausing.

'Casey not with you?' Darcie called after him.

He went into reverse. 'You'd be able to see her, if she was, wouldn't you? You can't see her, so she's not.'

The smiles fell from both their faces, to be replaced by surprise from Kelly and faint shock from Darcie. It gave him a small angry feeling in his guts. He made once more for the safety of his room, catching Kelly's muttered, 'Wow. He's gone into teenager mode, has he?'

And Darcie, sounding troubled. 'I think he's worried about his friend, Casey. She doesn't have a good time at home.'

Reversing sharply into the sitting room doorway once more, he speared his sister with a glare. 'What do you know about it?'

Slowly, Darcie's eyebrows rose, telling him that he was out of order. 'I know what you wanted me to know when you took me to see her home, Ross.'

His anger grew. Anger for Casey, anger at Casey. Unreasonably, he felt that Darcie was somehow contributing, sitting there in their nice warm house and talking to him with that teacherish note of warning in her voice. He didn't know whether to tell her about the incident with the rank old wino, whether she'd think worse of Casey for it. 'Well, you did fuck all about it, didn't you?' he snapped.

A heartbeat of silence. 'I don't think you ought to talk to me like that,' Darcie said, coolly. 'What would you like me to do?'

And he felt about ten again, inarticulate through swirling emotions. He wanted his mum and dad with a sudden fierce longing. Everyone else he knew had at least one of their parents around. It wasn't that he wasn't cool with Darcie. He was. But your sister wasn't meant to turn into your mum, trying to understand you when you felt like crap, telling you off when you acted out, giving you money and talking over your career options with you and vetting your friends. And telling you what constituted help and what constituted betrayal, when things were going badly for them.

Those were your mum's jobs.

Your sister should just be your sister, treating you like a nuisance sometimes and living her own life, and coming up with cool presents at Christmas. He and Darcie were equals, the same height on the family tree.

You shouldn't feel like such a shit when you made your sister feel bad. And she shouldn't make you feel bad when you were cold with misery, anyway. 'Just forget it,' he snapped.

11

Monday was one of Darcie's days off. Ross got up ready for school, face shuttered.

Hating the tension between them, Darcie gave him extra lunch money and a hug. 'You know, Ross, there's not much I can do about Casey's home life. Can't you get her to speak to a teacher, or someone? I'm not related to her. Anything I do will surely be seen as interference.'

He shot her a thoughtful glance, taking milk from the fridge. 'You don't even like her.'

'I don't know her,' she temporised. 'But if you're truly worried about her, you should suggest she asks for help from someone with a bit of power.'

He nodded, hesitated as if considering saying more but thinking better of it. 'Got to go.' And he left, leaning under the weight of his backpack as if it was stuffed with rocks.

Darcie pottered through the usual day-off chores, filling the washing machine, running the vacuum cleaner around, writing a shopping list. At the supermarket, she used the ATM, gathering up the crisp twenties and tens it disgorged. She must repay the £40 she owed Jake as soon as possible but he wouldn't be at the gallery shop today. She didn't know whether he was still surfing Kelly's sofa or whether he would have moved into Auntie Chrissy's house already.

It was as she was wheeling her trolley over the tarmac that she received a text message from Ross. The students absolutely were not allowed to take mobile phones into school, but it was a rule almost impossible to implement. She paused to read. *Casey not here. Not answering txts.* ☹

She answered. *Any of her friends heard from her?*

— *Nope. Think her dad might b hanging around*

— *Perhaps u should tell her form teacher u r worried?*

— *Dunno. Gotta go in now*

Darcie's route from Tesco to Eaton Walk took her down King's Road. On impulse, she diverted into the Blossom End estate, parking within sight of the house Ross had shown her. It wasn't hard to recognise, with its filthy net curtains and garden ornaments of discarded household appliances. She didn't really think that Casey would be in trouble.

But . . . what if she was?

She got out and crossed the green with a firm stride, her keys in her hand. The grass in front of the house had grown so tall it was beginning to fall over, exposing more rubbish. One window was still boarded up.

Darcie, trying to squash down an entire flight of butterflies swooping into her stomach, rapped at the door. After a pause a gaunt, grubby woman in a droopy T-shirt and washed out leggings opened it. She stared at Darcie owlishly.

'Mrs McClare?'

The woman frowned.

Darcie tried to be clearer. 'Are you Mrs McClare?'

'Me?' She retreated behind the door as if worried that Darcie would somehow force Mrs McClareness on her. 'No.'

A fat man slouched into the hall. He was even grubbier than the woman, shirt-front blotched with what looked like beer, worn and rubbed shiny trousers unfastened below a big belly. Darcie tried again. 'Mr McClare?'

With a sidelong glance at Darcie, the man addressed the woman. 'Woss she want?'

The woman shook her head again. 'Someone called McClare.'

'Woss she come here for?' The man turned and began to tread heavily up the ropy old stair-carpet. 'Tell her we ent go no McClares, so she can fuck off.'

Darcie made one last try before the door banged in her face. 'Are you Casey

McClare's mother?'

The woman shook her head again. 'Never heard of her.'

★   ★   ★

Darcie had gone home and unpacked her shopping in a haze, worries warring as to what to do next. Obviously, Ross had to know what had happened. But she felt a strong need for more facts. Casey must live somewhere. If not at the horrible home, then where? Why had she lied to Ross? The situation smelled of trouble. And Darcie preferred her to be the one to discover why, rather than find Ross up to his neck in something stinky.

She knew where Amy lived and that there wasn't much love lost between Amy and Casey. She went and parked in Amy's road to intercept her on her way home from school, feeling uncomfortably like a seedy private investigator. Finally Amy came wandering into view. She hesitated, warily, at finding Darcie lying in wait for her.

Darcie tried to sound casual, aware of the teenage habit of clamming up in response to an adult trying to get something on another kid. 'Hey, Amy. I'm trying to find Casey. I thought I knew where she lived but I've been to the wrong house today. Which court at Blossom End is it?'

Amy twirled her hair, thoughtfully. 'I don't know where she lives.'

'It's about a surprise for Ross,' Darcie said, encouragingly, economy with the truth being justified by her need to discover what Casey McClare was up to and whether Ross was likely to get hurt. 'That's why I can't ask him.'

Amy shrugged. 'My friend Layla should. They had to do an assignment together, once.' She dropped her bag onto the pavement and pulled out her phone and quickly made the call. When she rang off, she was frowning. 'Layla says she doesn't live at Blossom End. She's got it written on her Design folder: 22 First Avenue.'

Heart beginning to thump, Darcie said, 'Thanks.' First Avenue was in an older, OK bit of town, about a mile and a half away from Blossom End. 'I'll check it out.'

First Avenue was a street of red-brick semis. Number 22 had a trim lawn and a newish Volkswagen in the tiny drive.

Darcie ding-donged the door bell.

The woman who answered looked about forty. She wore the dress-and-jacket uniform of Murton's, an edge-of-town furniture store, and was fiddling with an earring. 'Yes?'

Darcie introduced herself. 'Is Casey McClare your daughter?'

The woman frowned, still battling with the earring. 'That's right. I'm Lynda McClare.'

O-kay . . . 'Ross Killengrey's my brother. May I have a chat with you about Casey?'

Wendy dropped her hands from her ear abruptly. 'You'd better come in.'

Darcie hesitated. 'Is Mr McClare here?'

'No.' Lynda McClare led the way

briskly into the sitting room, two rooms knocked into one then divided again by placing the sofa where the wall used to be. A good sofa, probably bought with Murton's staff discount, in a pleasant and comfy room. Darcie was having a hard time placing the wino Ross had described as Casey's dad in this pin-neat home.

Lynda regarded Darcie with a trace of hostility. 'I don't know any Ross whatever-you-said. What's he got to do with Casey? Did you say you're his sister?'

Darcie explained quickly that she was Ross's guardian, and why. 'Casey spends quite a bit of time at our house.'

'Casey's never mentioned him.' Wendy stared, a frown puckering her forehead like a pulled thread. 'She usually says she's at her friend Zoë's house, in the evenings.' She looked uncertain. 'So what's going on? Is she doing something at your house that she shouldn't?'

Darcie perched on the edge of a chair uneasily. 'No. She began to visit the house like any of Ross's friends. But recently he's become concerned for her.'

Lynda's hostility visibly increased. 'I can't get my head round this. Why would she lie about where she was? Why is he 'concerned' for her? Is Ross her boyfriend?'

'They're no more than close friends so far as I know.'

'I don't understand,' Lynda repeated.

They stared at each other across the neat, ordinary room. Cars swished by outside, birds sang in the shrubs. Darcie swallowed. 'Casey tells Ross that she has an underprivileged home life. That she lives in a filthy and dilapidated house in Blossom End with a mother who can't cope, and she's had trouble with her father.'

Lynda gaped. 'Her father? What kind of trouble could she have with him?'

Darcie felt her colour rise. She tried to make her tone neutral. 'She says he's abusive and lies in wait for her.'

'But it's total rubbish!' Lynda jumped to her feet. 'And you say all this information comes from Casey?'

Rising warily, Darcie jammed her hands in her pockets. 'Sorry. But that's what she says.'

A silence. Then, Mrs McClare gave a half-laugh. 'Casey hasn't got a father.' Another silence. Lynda lit a cigarette, noisily, with a match, striking it with a big *zzzipppp* and tilting her head extravagantly to suck in the flame. She blew a stream of smoke. 'Or, at least, not one she knows. He left. A baby was too much responsibility for him.' She smoked silently for a minute, alternately staring at the floor and Darcie.

'I'm due at work,' she said, eventually. 'I'll have to ring in sick.' She'd become so pale that her saleswoman's make-up stood out like a mask. Darcie hovered whilst Lynda rang her supervisor and then made mugs of strong coffee. 'Casey's been a storyteller all her life, but this just about takes the biscuit. God, what am I going to do with her?' She drew on a fresh cigarette as if trying to inhale it whole. 'I'm afraid I know why she's doing all this attention seeking. It's Freddie.'

'Freddie?'

Lynda crushed out her cigarette. 'He's my boyfriend. Has been for five years, but Casey hates even the sound of his name. If Freddie walks in the door, Casey walks out — which is why she spends so much time 'at Zoë's'. I talk and talk to her about the situation and that I'm entitled to a life, but . . . I don't know if she's got some hazy idea that if I stay single her dad'll turn up one day.' She laughed, bitterly. 'He won't. And if he did she'd be in for a sad disappointment. He's a loser.'

Any reply Darcie might have made was interrupted by the opening of the front door and Casey's voice loud in the hall.

Darcie and Lynda waited in silence as Casey and a woman in her thirties strolled in, laughing together, hands linked, the woman asking, 'This boy who's got the stuff, how much has he sold?'

When they saw their reception

committee, they froze. The woman had the same sooty eye make-up and black-dyed hair as Casey, and wore a black embroidered dress.

Lynda jumped up. 'Casey, who the bloody hell's this?'

The woman swung on her heel and hurried from the house.

Lynda groped behind herself and dropped down into her chair again, her hair falling over her pallid forehead. 'Who is she, Casey? She must be thirty-five, what the hell are you doing acting so chummy with her? And why haven't you been to school?'

Casey glanced behind herself as if considering scooting out after her friend. Then she glared at Darcie and rolled her eyes. 'If she's found her smart-arse way here then you probably know most of it.' She flopped down in an armchair and folded her arms.

Tears trickled down Lynda's pale cheeks as she accused Casey of all the lies Darcie had uncovered, Casey shrugging, sneering, studying her nails and not meeting anyone's eyes. Darcie would've liked to escape but Ross's involvement made it sensible to hang on in case there was anything she needed to know.

Casey's defence centred around, 'I told a few porkies. Better than hanging around while you have a disgusting relationship with your disgusting old-man-friend.'

Wiping her eyes on her sleeve, Lynda choked, 'I'm allowed a boyfriend.'

Then it was Casey who was shouting, 'And I'm allowed to hate him, right?'

Tears rolled faster down poor Lynda's face. 'What's he ever done to you?'

Casey went back to examining her nails. 'Nothing. I wish he had, I could report him and get him out of our life.'

'You wicked little bitch,' whispered Lynda. 'And you haven't told me who that woman is?'

That was when Casey looked up, her eyes full of spite. 'That's my Zoë,' she purred. 'She's my friend. *My very special friend.* Geddit?'

'I thought Zoë was a girl from school. And you were holding hands — '

'Loads of people are gay, Mum. Don't sweat it.'

Lynda shrank into her chair. 'At your age? You're hardly old enough to know . . . And she's so much older.'

Casey looked up at a big black wall clock. 'Why aren't you at work, anyway? You're always at work. That's all you do, late nights, Sundays. It's nice I've done something to make you stop.'

Lynda's pallor had become frightening. 'I always notice you, Casey. I rang in sick when I heard what Darcie had to say.'

Casey threw Darcie another filthy look and all but hissed at her.

Darcie decided she'd had enough. She wasn't learning anything new and Casey's twisted young life was making her faintly nauseous.

'I'd better go. It doesn't seem as if any of this is relevant to Ross.'

Casey smirked.

12

Telling Ross was hell.

Bewilderment and hurt warred in his face as Darcie explained; his eyes pleaded for it not to be true. 'But I used to walk her home — up to Blossom End!'

Stroking his hand across the kitchen table, heart clenching for his pain, Darcie said, 'I expect she waited until you'd gone and then made off to her real home. She just seems to have enjoyed living a lie. Her mum says it's attention seeking.'

'And you say this Zoë friend is a woman? In her thirties?'

'That's what she looked like.'

'Bitch,' he breathed. 'She told me she didn't like to be touched. Why couldn't she just tell me that she's gay?'

Darcie squeezed his hand. 'She probably got off on you being attracted to her. It gave her a feeling of power.

Certainly, something was pleasing her, judging from her smug expression.'

Dismay flickered across Ross's young face before he managed to shutter the expression. And Darcie wished bed bugs and boils on Casey McClare.

*   *   *

Ross hung around outside the school until he spotted Ben's bulky figure getting off the bus. 'Hey.'

Ben said, 'Hey,' but didn't slow, and Ross had to turn and fall in step beside him.

'Got a big problem.' Ross lowered his voice. 'You know those phones and things I've been selling for Casey — I think they might be stolen.'

Ben made a goofy face. 'Wow, what a shock!'

Ross had to trot a couple of strides through the school gate so as not to lose him in the early morning crush to get to registration before the second bell. 'You think they are, then?'

Ben stopped in the middle of the quad and turned to face Ross squarely. 'Of course they are! I reckon that phone Casey sold me was my own. She stole it, gave it new buttons from some cheap facia then sold me it back and, like a mug, I fell for it. And then there was that thing with her dad ... ' He shuddered. 'She's such bad news.'

Ben joined the jostle of black sweatshirted shoulders trying to force themselves through the main door of the humanities block.

Shouldering gamely at his side, at an advantage as one of the tallest, Ross demanded, 'Why didn't you say?'

Ben shook his head. 'Ross, you acted like you were her pet monkey.' He jostled harder as the second bell went and Ross slowed, letting him go ahead.

He didn't go to registration. He didn't go to first lesson. Instead, he went to the window at school reception. 'Can I see Mr Able straight away, please?' he said to the office lady who had thick glasses and lipstick on her teeth. 'It's urgent.' He took a seat on a blue chair outside the head teacher's room.

After a few minutes, the lady from the office, visibly irritated that she'd had to leave her cosy office and walk twenty yards up the carpeted corridor, paused by Ross's chair. 'Mr Able says, will you try him again at lunch time? He's got something on at the moment.'

Ross sat back in the chair, a low, square thing without arms. 'It's *urgent*.'

With a cluck, she disappeared again, returning after several minutes, smoothing open the pages of a diary. 'I'm to make you an appointment for later, Mr Able says.'

Ross shook his head, looking blankly past her. 'I'll wait here.'

The lady from the office glared. 'He can't see you!'

Ross turned to give her glare for glare. 'Look, I'm in full school uniform, even the shoes, my tie's done up, so's my top button, there's no writing on my hand, no visible obscenity on the badges on my bag, I'm not chewing gum. I'm not adopting a hostile tone of voice. I'm doing everything right, here. I've got something really important to tell Mr Able. He'll want to know. I swear he will.'

She eyed him. He eyed her back. She tried, 'How about you go to your Head of Year?'

He shook his head and began to ignore her.

He sat on the blue chair for an hour and twenty-five minutes, staring straight ahead, his bag between his feet, the shoulder strap loosely in his hand. His brain churned. Was Casey in school? How would she be when their paths collided? Maybe she'd just blank him like Amy did when they split up. She might sneer or even come up with excuses for what she'd done. No doubt Unsad Zag was the mastermind behind it all.

At least he didn't care any more.

The crying, the fury that had sent him to his room to punch impotently at his pillows until his arms shook? That was so over.

Now he was going to do that thing Darcie sometimes talked about. Damage limitation.

'If it's *so* urgent you'd better come in, but I'm waiting for someone so be quick!'

Ross looked up. Mr Able was standing in the doorway of his room, wearing a harassed frown with his highly-polished shoes. As Ross followed him into his office he realised he was now sufficient inches taller than Mr Able to see that his blond hair was thinning fast.

Once in the office, he cut across the head teacher's opening plea for clarity and brevity by taking from his backpack a carrier bag, which he emptied gently across the desk.

Mr Able halted mid-sentence to gaze at the array of mobile phones.

'This is what I need to talk to you about.' Ross took a huge breath. 'I think I've been tricked into selling these phones by Casey McClare. And I think they might be stolen.'

And that's when the office lady with

lipsticky teeth knocked and bustled through the door, saying, 'The police are here, Mr Able. You said to bring them straight in.'

Shit. Shit, shit, shit! Heart curling, Ross gazed in horror at Mr Able, and then at the policemen blocking the doorway.

The leading police constable, tapping his fingers against his body armour as he gazed at the booty on the desk, raised his eyebrows.

Ross let his head fall back in frustration. 'Bastard. She's dobbed me in before I can dob her.'

★　★　★

Ross felt as if he'd shifted to an alternate reality, being taken down to the police station and formally arrested. His interview with the police seemed to go on forever and took place in the presence of Darcie, who'd raced to the station as if summoned by the devil, her face paper-white, gazing at Ross as if he'd shed a skin and become someone quite unrecognisable. Also, almost unbelievably, there was someone the policeman called a duty lawyer, Mrs Sharman, who wore a blue suit and carried a black case.

Ross could see Darcie shaking as she took the seat beside his in a room painted white and kept too cool. Maybe it was the chill that made her shiver. Or maybe it was the fear Ross was sure he must be giving off, like a bad smell. 'I'm sorry, Darce,' he said. 'Casey totally took me in.'

★   ★   ★

Darcie managed a tiny frozen smile and took his hand as if he were still five and Mum had asked her to take him to the shop. She tried to think what Mum would have done — Mum who had seemed always to know what to do in every situation. She shook herself. 'I know.' She tried to make her smile broader and more reassuring before turning to

Mrs Sharman. 'Ross has never been in trouble in his life.'

Mrs Sharman nodded. 'Let's start with you telling me the story of how you came to be in the police station this morning, Ross.'

So Ross told everything to Mrs Sharman whilst Darcie tried to keep herself from leaping in with loud demands for the blood of Casey McClare. Then the dark-haired policeman, stolid in his blue uniform, took him over, up, down sideways and over again how he'd been selling stolen phones to school kids. Using Ross's name every few words, he listened as Ross insisted that he hadn't known the goods were stolen because he'd asked, and been assured they weren't. Mrs Sharman emphasised this point, and that he'd been in the act of asking his head teacher for help when the police turned up.

The policeman looked levelly at him. 'And where did you think the phones and things came from, Ross?'

Ross looked levelly back. 'She said a mate of hers reconditioned stuff. His name's Colin Jones.'

'And do you know Colin, Ross? Have you met him?'

'No. Casey just brought stuff she said he'd reconditioned.' He told them about Ben's phone, that Ben had complained about it this morning, and Ross had come immediately to report to Mr Able.

It was an endless, ugly session, and Ross had to ask twice to be allowed to go to the toilet.

Finally, the policeman told Darcie to take Ross home. At home, Darcie rang Mr Able and was told that Ross would not be allowed back into school until further notice. He had to make his own enquiries but this was a serious matter. It was not the kind of thing he'd tolerate occurring in his school.

The police had just returned to school and taken Casey McClare to the police station.

★   ★   ★

137

Ross was silent, shut in his room. When Darcie looked in on him he was sitting on his bed staring into space with furious concentration. Darcie didn't see much point in insisting on talking. She'd heard the whole unbelievable thing recounted for the benefit of the lawyer and the police.

What was she supposed to do? Dealing with Ross being made a stool pigeon wasn't in the Good Guardian's Handbook. Not that she had a copy. But she couldn't possibly return to work as if nothing had happened. Round and round whirled her thoughts as she curled on the sofa, drank coffee and nursed a sinking feeling worthy of the Titanic.

Ross's word against Casey's.

Casey getting in first with her claim that Ross had been stealing and selling.

Darcie had a horrible feeling that Casey's version actually sounded more likely than Ross's convoluted tale of innocence and gullibility.

After two cups of coffee she saw they

were running low on milk and seized on it as an excuse for brief escape, shouting up the stairs, 'I'm going to the shop. Back in ten minutes.' Wriggling into her jacket, she strode off down the street, glad to let the breeze blow through her mind.

★ ★ ★

Jake sat in an armchair that seemed to smell faintly of Darcie's perfume. Ross was sprawled on the sofa, his young face white and haunted. 'So the little cow's stitched me up,' Ross said.

Jake heard the back door open and close, then Darcie was standing in the doorway, staring across the room at him, looking only slightly less pale and stressed than Ross.

'And I'm excluded from school while the police and Mr Able make enquiries — but at least the cops have hauled her in, too,' Ross added, with vicious satisfaction.

Jake made his voice matter of fact.

'Sounds like Casey was a cat's paw to this woman, Zoë. Casey had a crush on her and she used that for her own ends.'

'And Casey used me just the same, the bitch.'

Jake smiled at Darcie. 'Sorry to barge in. But when you rushed off, leaving your workshop unlocked, everyone was worried that something horrible had happened and you haven't replied to texts or calls, so I thought I'd better check you out. Stu's manning the shop.'

Darcie came in and flopped down onto the sofa beside Ross, a white plastic milk bottle hooked over one finger. 'Ross has obviously told you why I was called away, so it is pretty horrible. We've been stuck down at the cop shop. I turned my phone to silent while Ross gave his statement.' She fished her phone out of the pocket of her jeans. 'Oops. I've got a load of missed call notifications.'

'Anything I can do?'

Suddenly, Darcie's eyes glittered with tears. She swallowed. 'You could lock my workshop for me. I won't be back today.'

'Already done. Auntie Chrissy left me the spare workshop keys, all neatly labelled.' His smile was faint. 'Anything else? Or do you just want to be left alone to feel bloody?'

This time, she just nodded.

Jake hoisted himself to his feet and clapped Ross on the shoulder. 'Try and put it down to experience and hope the police can pin it on Casey the Bitch.'

'Yeah. Thanks,' said Ross, gruffly. Then, to Darcie. 'I'm going to ring Amy and ask if she's heard if the police let Casey go.' And he made for the sanctuary of his own room.

Jake watched him go. He smiled at Darcie, his heart going out to her. 'I don't think I completely appreciated the extent of your responsibility for your brother, till now. It's huge.'

She smiled tiredly and got up to see him out. 'And soooooo much fun. The head teacher gave me a lecture on the phone about backing up the school by

141

grounding Ross for the duration of his exclusion. Which is the kind of thing that's really difficult to implement when you're not actually the parent. Then the git seemed to read my mind and started talking about seeking support or even counselling.'

'Rather you than me,' said Jake, sympathetically. He wanted to pull her into his arms, to feel her sag against him and accept his strength and comfort, to stroke her hair and kiss away the strain from every inch of her face.

But Darcie stepped back, as if she read his intent in his eyes. 'That's what they all say.'

13

Darcie was washing up from a dinner that neither she nor Ross had eaten much of, wishing that Kelly hadn't picked these few days to be sent on a training jolly on the south coast. The doorbell rang and she opened the front door with suds on her hands to see Jake standing there with a bottle of Bailey's in one hand and a box of cornflakes in the other.

Despite her misery, she giggled. 'You really know how to show a girl a good time.'

'Glad you remembered.' He stepped into the hall. 'How's Ross?'

'Brooding.'

'Can't blame him. He got the shitty end of the stick.'

She took him into the kitchen. 'I don't think I said it earlier but thank you for locking the workshop and coming to check on me. It's been such a crappy day. And, whilst I remember . . . ' She took the forty pounds she owed him from her purse, which was lying on the worktop. 'Thanks.' She managed a smile. 'I haven't got much appetite for the Cornflakes. But I do have some ice.'

He pulled out a kitchen chair and folded himself into it. 'Bring it on.'

She wiped out two of her mum's crystal tumblers, remembering, with a pang, how Mum had insisted that all drinks tasted better from crystal or china than plain old glass or pottery, and began to wrestle with an ice tray from the freezer. 'Somebody ought to invent ice trays that will give up the ice cubes without a fight.' She tried in vain, to twist the frozen plastic into submission.

He took the tray from her with a Popeye flexing of his arm. 'It needs a man.'

'And you're the closest we've got?' The friendly insult fell naturally from her tongue as if they were still Ross's age, before there had been anything between them. Before that hot night in Jake's bed. Before that deadly cold argument the next day. Before the growth of the tension that seemed to have accompanied so many of their conversations since Jake's return.

Jake just laughed, turned two ice cubes into each of the tumblers and watching as she slowly poured the liqueur over, like pale chocolate milk.

They took their drinks through to the sitting room sofa and Jake lifted his glass to her in a toast, eyes narrowed and glittering in the pool of light thrown by the floor lamp.

And something went *boi-oingggggg!* in Darcie's chest. Oh no! She drained her glass, very conscious of Jake doing the same.

He moved closer, until they were touching. Darcie felt as if a giant was walking past, making the ground shake and her body pulse to its footsteps. Jake's warm fingers found hers, linked.

His mouth was very near and she let herself think happy thoughts about lying on dewy evening grass, his mouth on hers, the air jumping with promise. When she'd ached, and enjoyed aching.

With a superhuman effort she slipped her fingers free.

Leaning his elbow on the sofa back and propping his head on his hand, he blew out a sigh. 'Oh. So we're just going to carry on pretending there's nothing between us, are we?'

Silently, she nodded.

He let the silence stretch. Then, 'I was wrong to snap at you, the other day, when you wanted to talk. Can we talk now? Or,' he ran his knuckle down her bare forearm, 'we could do as I suggest and just put the bad stuff behind us. Why don't we go out on a few dates and see how things go? Then we could progress to dinner at my place — well, Auntie Chrissy's place.'

Darcie knew where Chrissy lived, of course, in a row of little houses that had somehow missed being knocked down as the town centre grew, and still nestled behind the shops on the High Street. For a moment she allowed herself to think about secreting herself there with Jake for a cosy evening and her heart leapt. But then she caught hold of it and pressed it firmly back into its proper place. Ross. A 'huge responsibility', Jake had called him. Better believe it, buddy. 'Rather you than me.' OK. She could understand why he'd feel like that. But she wasn't sure what kind of a dating future she could have with someone who did.

She got up, retrieved the bottle of Bailey's from the kitchen, refilled both drinks and clinked glasses with him before she answered. 'Today's been such a bad day, Jake.' She didn't feel up to any further explanations, so she began to talk about Welbourne Workshops, instead.

His smile died, but he didn't argue.

14

Ross was excluded from school until he'd been back to the police station, two weeks later, once again in the company of Darcie and Mrs Sharman.

There, to his huge relief, the policeman told him that they weren't going to take the matter any further. 'Your bacon was saved by you already being in the act of coming clean with your head teacher when we arrived on the scene. His statement, and that of your mate, Benjamin Bloor, corroborate your story. You've been a bit innocent and gullible, and we're all hoping you'll be a bit more cautious another time.'

Through a hot rush of dizziness, Ross heard Darcie sort of sigh and gulp beside him. 'So — is that it?' he managed.

The policeman smiled. 'Just watch yourself, mate. It's too easy to be drawn into situations. Hopefully you've learned from this.'

'Absolutely,' said Ross, politely, because all he wanted was to be allowed to get out of the scary clinical confines of the police station and never go back. Except he just had one last question . . . 'And what about Casey?'

The policeman closed the file in front of him. 'We'd like a witness statement from you about that and I plan to phone you in a few days to arrange to visit you at home.' He glanced at Darcie. 'And if you could be present, as Ross's responsible adult?'

Darcie hesitated. 'Does Ross have to?'

'I want to,' stuck in Ross, indignantly.

'We can't insist,' the policeman answered Darcie. 'But Ross is in a good position to help us.'

Ross butted in before Darcie could come up with a reason for him not to make a statement. 'Will Casey know?'

'At some point, yes, she will be made aware of all the evidence against her.'

Delight licked around his bruised

heart. 'Wicked. I'll do it.'

Beside him, Darcie sighed again.

The next day, Mr Able allowed him back into school, after a serious talk with him and Darcie, which Ross hated, because what had Darce done wrong? He was sentenced to a whole month of 'school service' — picking up litter or running errands for teachers during breaks.

'You're a bright boy, Ross,' said Mr Able, over the steeple of his fingers. 'You ought to have applied your intelligence to the Casey situation, not gone into it with your eyes shut. I don't expect any repetition, all right? I don't want to have to exclude you permanently.' He gave him a long, pensive stare.

'Am I allowed to ask what happened to Casey?' Darcie ventured, as Mr Able got to his feet to signify the end of the interview. They knew from Amy that Casey hadn't been back to school since the police took her away.

'Miss McClare was excluded, just as Ross was. I'm afraid I couldn't comment further.'

★   ★   ★

Darcie spent the next two weeks feeling flat and uncreative. Knowing better than to work on anything sumptuous and large — which would cost her a lot of money if cocked up — she spent her time making coasters and dinner mats with various designs and transfers on the underside. She probably wouldn't have to make anything else so dreary for months and, hopefully, soon she'd feel her usual self. The police had been and taken Ross's witness statement about young Casey's crafty activities, so that was one thing off her mind, anyway. And, by the grin on Ross's face, giving evidence against Casey had satisfied a deep need for revenge.

On Friday lunchtime, she was momentarily cheered when Kelly burst in through the door, face pink and beaming, waving a paper bag stuffed with goodies from the baguette shop. 'Tarrah! I have lunch! I have great news. Which would you like first?'

Hugging her in the pure pleasure of seeing a happy face, Darcie decided, 'The good news, obviously. No, wait until I've made the coffee. Then you can splurge.' She boiled the kettle whilst Kelly split the paper bags as a makeshift tablecloth and laid out the crusty baguettes and flapjacks on a stool, filling the workshop with the smell of onion and cucumber.

Darcie dragged up another stool for the coffee mugs, and settled onto an old dining chair. 'Go on then. Tell.'

Kelly let her eyes half-close in bliss. 'I've met a really nice man, called Simon. We were on the train together when I'd been to a work thing in London. We talked for the entire journey. He's single, just come back to England after working in Australia for a while. He's living in Middledip and commuting, because he doesn't mind working in London but doesn't want to live there. Once we realised we were getting out at the same station he asked me out to dinner, last night. And we had such a good time and he's so lovely! We're going to the cinema tonight. He's a Star Wars fan and they're showing one of the episodes in 3D, then we're going for pizza. He's the original 'tall, dark and handsome' and we can just talk for hours . . . '

Darcie, finishing her baguette, waited politely to be offered a flapjack. But Kelly, baguette dangling from her fingers, was still eulogising, eyes sparkling, mouth one continuous smile. Of course, Darcie was thrilled for Kelly that she was soaring high on a cloud of instant-attraction joy. But, within the warm fuzzies for her friend, she was conscious of a chilly yesterday's-rice-pudding feeling for herself. Kelly had plans for tonight, tomorrow night and most of the weekend. Any ideas Darcie might have had of unloading her deflated feelings on Kelly over an Indian take-away and a couple of bottles of wine looked to be redundant.

But, come on, this was *Kelly*, her best friend, dizzily pouring out Simon's life history with a touchingly possessive pride. She put down her coffee cup and flung her arms around her friend once more. 'He sounds gorgeous, Kelly. I hope you have a fantastic time.'

★ ★ ★

A great thing about Auntie Chrissy's house was its location. Jake could reach any town-centre pub or club in minutes. To distract himself from the knowledge that Darcie had gone all distant on him he decided to call in at The Golden Lion for a few drinks. His old buddies from school still hung out there and a few beers and a bit of mindless banter might disperse the lead he felt he carried in his belly.

He'd reached the end of Pebble Lane where it joined the main road, with all its traffic noise and babble, when a figure seemed to hurtle towards him through the air, landing with a thud and a cry on the pavement at his feet. He leaped back, looking up to see a noisy line of teenagers straggling up the iron staircase to a club, gazing down at the figure on the floor. And three lads racing down the steps, fists clenched, their intentions towards the prone figure written on their faces.

The figure groaned and began to lever himself up, blood spattering on the paving.

'*Ross?*' The instant Jake recognised Darcie's little brother, he acted, grabbing a bamboo cane from the flower tub outside the last house in the lane and stepping across Ross to face his pursuers.

The three halted. Jake flexed the cane, unspeaking.

One lad lurched forward. 'Get out of the way.'

Behind him, Jake heard Ross gasp. He waited until the lad came within range and released one end of the bamboo. It hissed through the air and swiped the lad's ear with a vicious slap, making him rear back on a howl of pain.

Jake smiled at the others. 'I think it's time you guys disappeared.' He swished the cane at their groins a couple of times and the lads jumped back. 'Bye bye,' he said.

*　　*　　*

Bookwork, bookwork, Darcie hated it. But Ross was out mending fences with Ben and Jonny and Kelly was no doubt snuggling down with her lovely man and a box of popcorn, so she planted herself on the sofa and booted up her laptop, preparing to have yet another go at her spreadsheets, and trying not to think how much she would rather have been watching Star Wars in 3D with a lovely man.

She had a reasonable run at inputting the first quarter's invoices, but then her mood sunk lower than ever when she realised she'd left the second quarter's invoices at the workshop. It was with relief that she heard the back door opening and she stretched, heart lightening. Ross was home. Maybe they could share a cup of hot chocolate and watch South Park . . . she paused to listen. Ross talking to someone. Well, OK, Ben and Jonny would probably be up for South Park, too. She could put some twisty fries in the oven and — But Ross was sounding funny, muffled, as if he'd just had a filling.

'Hanks a yot,' she heard him say. 'Yeah, I'll be ohay now, I'll be fine, honest. Hanks again. No, I'll tell her.'

She jumped up and zipped into the kitchen just in time to see Ross preparing to show Jake out. And then he turned round.

Darcie clapped her hands to her mouth. 'Oh *Ross*, what happened?' She started forward, turning him under the light to examine his face. His lip was split and swollen, blood had run down and made his chin rusty. The area around one eye was bright red and puffed up. 'Look at the state of you! Sit down, let's get you cleaned up and get some ice on it.'

Ross let himself be urged to a kitchen chair.

'I gock pushed downstairs,' he mumbled.

Darcie halted, her hands full of wet kitchen roll. 'What? Who?'

He shrugged. 'Some glokes. I landed on my face. Yake came ayong and saw them off before they could do any more.'

Darcie began to dab yards of kitchen paper to his bloody face.

'Yake Gelfast. Gelly's gother,' Ross clarified, as if Darcie couldn't see Jake closing the back door again with himself on the inside of it.

'I think he ought to go to A and E,' he said, softly.

Darcie sighed, seeing the thick split in her brother's lip beading with fresh blood. 'You're right.'

Though thanking Jake profusely, Darcie refused his offer to accompany them to casualty, because it was so much easier forgetting how she felt about him when not with him, then

158

spent a couple of hours in Bettsbrough General waiting for someone to stitch Ross up. He endured, stoically, first the long wait with soggy kitchen roll and ice pressed against his lips, the melted ice mixing with the blood and dripping pinkly onto the tiled waiting area, and then the actual needlework.

During the wait, Darcie interrogated him, but he couldn't shed much light on what had happened.

Ross, Ben and Jonny had been at the top of the steps up to Benny's, the under-18s nightclub over a parade of shops in the town centre, someone jostled Ross and then shoved violently — and he'd been airborne until he bounced off the handrail and hit the ground in Pebble Lane. 'They ran down after me, but Jake was in the street and he got this bamboo stick from somewhere and let one of them have it. So they legged it.' Ross's speech was becoming clearer as the ice brought the swelling down.

Darcie went cold. If Ross had

received the full dose of what was intended for him, it could've been serious.

Ross pulled his bloody, almost-melted icepack from his lips and inspected the gory mess. 'Unlucky for them that Jake was there. Man, he fights dirty, doesn't he? Dead wicked.'

Darcie felt her heart somersault. She'd hardly had time yet to examine the knowledge that Jake had saved Ross. 'I do seem to remember that capability coming in useful, sometimes,' she admitted.

Ross grinned and then winced and hurriedly reapplied his icepack. 'He wanted to call the ambulance but I was OK, really.'

Darcie buried her face in her hands.

★   ★   ★

Apart from the horrible period of his parents' accident, when the coppers had been kind and supportive, Ross'd had nothing to do with the police. Now it was beginning to be a habit. He faced two more police officers over his kitchen table. At least this time he was clearly the victim, unless the police suspected him of throwing himself down the stairs ahead of those guys and so Darcie was less tense. Last time, she'd been stretched so tight he'd expected her to go 'ping'.

He had nothing against the police for telling him off about those phones because it was obvious that they could have put him in far deeper shit. But they were pretty boring. Same questions over and over, then they'd write it all down and read it to him, and he had to sign in all kinds of places on the sheets of paper, and Darcie had to sign in too, and it was all just too dull. And it reminded him of the black cloud that had hung over him, making him feel sick and squirmy inside.

But he'd agreed to see them because it was obvious Casey set the sneaky bastard stair pushers on him. And he wanted to pay Casey back.

A lot of his waking thoughts were concerned with paying Casey back. He'd lie awake, planning.

He. Would. Pay. Casey. Back.

★ ★ ★

Summer sun shone low through the open door of Darcie's unit, glinting through the light-catchers she was making. Light-catchers made affordable little reminders of a nice day out for customers to hang in their windows, marginally less boring to produce than coasters.

The one she was working on was circular, a clear background with an orange-and-yellow sun surrounded by bevelled, pointy rays. The next would be a crescent moon with a star, to encourage customers to buy the pair. She was chuffed with the way the affordable stuff was making money but would be so glad to get onto her next commission, an intricate panel destined to become part of a window between two rooms in a posh apartment in Peterborough.

On the bench beside the light-catchers sat a small pair of cufflinks, dark grey glass, faceted painstakingly by hand on the grinding wheel and polished, each one etched with a J, on sterling silver mounts she'd ordered as part of a trial she was going to run into glass jewellery, which should be both affordable and desirable. And more fun to make than coasters.

She scooped up the cufflinks and went home to get changed.

★   ★   ★

From the bedroom window Jake caught sight of her coming up Pebble Lane, placing each foot deliberately, like a stalking cat. She wore a denim jacket against the cool of the day and the breeze blew her hair all over one shoulder.

She paused in front of the house.

He waited for her knock. He waited

163

so long that he wondered if she'd somehow crept away without him seeing. He forgot to breathe, and his chest began to hurt.

But finally . . . there it was, a little tattoo. He took in some air. Be cool, be cool, count to five before answering. One. Two. Thr — That would do.

★   ★   ★

The door opened. Jake looked surprised to see her, but smiled his slow smile in welcome. She'd say her piece, she thought, and be on her way.

But he turned and walked away from the open door, saying over his shoulder as if assuming that she'd intended to go in, 'I'm just making a drink. At the spa they used to make this fantastic lemon tea and I had a sudden yen for it.'

If she wanted to say anything, it seemed she'd have to follow. Stepping into the cool, white-painted simplicity of the little house, she closed the door behind her.

'Go into the lounge, won't be a minute,' he called back from the kitchen.

She tensed as she heard his footsteps returning. Any moment now she'd be able to begin her speech.

Then he was there with two large, clear glass cups, like bowls with handles, full of amber liquid that reflected the light from the window. 'Sit down.' He passed her one of the cups; the contents smelt delicious, lemon and cinnamon, sharp and steamy.

Auntie Chrissy's lounge had no chairs, just one of those huge corner sofas with a chaise end, so Darcie had no option but to sit on the same piece of furniture as Jake. She blew across the surface of her drink, sipped, swallowed. Her throat smouldered. 'The fantastic kind of lemon tea with whisky in it?'

One corner of his mouth twitched. 'Schnapps.'

'Seems like a Jake drink.' She opened her mouth again to begin her speech. 'What I've come for — '

'How's Ross?'

She wished he'd let her get this vote of thanks over with! 'OK really, but he looks beautiful. His lips are swollen, he's got two stitches in one, and a black eye.'

Jake grimaced. 'The police gave me a call to arrange to take a statement confirming Ross's story. They don't seem to think they'll get anywhere, though, with neither of us being able to identify the guys.'

She sipped her drink as he recounted the conversation. The lemon was sharp on her tongue, the after-kick of the schnapps rolled down her throat. The cup was heavy and had even begun to make her hands sweat a little; she had to put it down to wriggle out of her jacket as the alcohol flushed warmth through her.

Then, finally, she got the opportunity to launch. 'I came to thank you for helping Ross. I'm incredibly grateful, it hardly bears thinking about what would've happened if you hadn't waded in.' She closed her eyes for a moment as if in silent agony at the idea, but really because his gaze had sent a swoosh down her spine, and she felt he could too easily read it. She cleared her throat. 'It was no small thing you did, pitching in when the odds were against you.'

'I had surprise on my side, along with that handy bit of bamboo. Just as well, because I didn't like the idea of getting clouted.'

She laughed. 'Well, we're both hugely grateful, thank you. And I — I've got something for you.' She fumbled in the top pocket of her shirt and brought out the cufflinks. Her hand shook slightly as she let the cufflinks roll gently from her palm to his.

He studied them for several moments, revolving them between his fingers. 'Did you make these?'

She nodded.

'For me?'

'Yes.'

'Cool. They're excellent.'

She flushed. 'It was a pretty cool thing you did.'

'And quite a nice thank you.' He leaned closer, making her wonder . . . Then, slowly, he pulled open her pocket, and tipped the cufflinks back in. She jumped at the sensation of them tumbling over her breast like two tiny mice. 'But that's not the thank you I want.' He smiled.

It must be the schnapps. Darcie was actually on fire. Could scarcely lubricate her throat enough to speak. 'What — ?'

His eyes fixed on her mouth. 'I want a kiss.'

She licked dry lips, tried a laugh, which came out squeaky.

His eyes never left her face. 'Kiss me. Because you know you want to.'

She looked at his lips. Sexy, full lips, soft and smooth. Her own felt dry and rough.

'Darcie, come on.' His voice was no more than a breath, but it somehow trickled down her neck, her back, spreading like hot treacle.

She sighed, and leaned forward,

feeling her eyes close gently as her mouth found his, as his tongue touched hers, as they tasted each other again. A gentle, languorous kiss. Then Jake's mouth grew more insistent and he pulled her into his arms.

'Ow!' The cufflinks in Darcie's pocket jabbed her soft flesh.

'Whoops.' Jake delved delicately into the pocket, touching her breast through the fabric of her shirt, removed the cufflinks and balanced them on the arm of the sofa. Then he climbed to his feet and pulled her up and into his arms, all in one movement. His hands dropped to cup her buttocks and pull her groin deliciously against his. She kissed him, nipping his lower lip.

He murmured against her mouth, 'I have wanted you so much and for so long.'

She groaned. 'Me, too.'

The ridiculously narrow stairs were a challenge for two people to climb side by side, but a stumbling kind of progress was possible if the two people were twined tightly enough around each other to slide between the walls. Undressing became a game of mobile, vertical twister. They reached the bedroom and nakedness at roughly the same time. For a moment they just held on.

Then Jake's hands were tracing the bones of her back, his mouth touching her lips, her throat, her breasts, until she could only breathe in gasps, her body arching towards him, pulling him closer.

And when he entered her she experienced a spasm so intense that for several seconds she stopped breathing altogether, craving his body, the feel, the taste. When she cried out he was watching her face, and she thought she'd never seen anything so erotically beautiful as the blaze of hunger in his eyes. She wished that life were so simple that he could stay inside her forever, and she'd be utterly happy.

★ ★ ★

On Saturday afternoon, Ross walked to the Wellbourne Workshops, having decided that if he did the right thing without being told it might make Darcie happy. He'd been a lot of trouble to Darcie lately. Being off school hadn't been as much fun as he might have thought; teachers had sent home tons of course work because he had his GCSEs next year. Being shoved downstairs had been even less fun but at least being back in school allowed his mates to see him before he healed. A black eye looked so cool.

The door to Darcie's workshop stood open and he trod softly in. 'I've come up to thank Jake for what he did.'

She jumped, almost dropping a cardboard box in her arms. 'Ross!' Then, recovering from his sudden appearance, as he'd hoped, she looked pleased. 'OK. I've already thanked him. But I'm sure he'd appreciate you doing it yourself. I'm about to take these lampshades over to him for the shop.'

'I'll help.' Ross stacked the first four

boxes on the big wooden sack barrow that Darcie used on such occasions and manoeuvred it carefully over the steps, because it had a mind of its own, while Darcie warned, 'Remember that stuff's delicate,' and went ahead to open the shop door.

As she stepped inside he heard her say, 'Ross's here. He's manning the sack barrow for me.'

By the time Ross had manhandled the wayward barrow in, Jake was on his way over to receive the boxes, each labelled in Darcie's loopy handwriting, *affordable geometric red* or *affordable geometric green*. 'That eye's pretty impressive.'

Ross grinned. 'Doesn't hurt much now, unless you press it.' He pushed it with his fingertip and grimaced, to illustrate his point. 'Thanks again for helping me out. I was definitely outnumbered.'

'Guys like that wouldn't have it any other way. The police haven't been able to pin any involvement on your old friend, Casey, then?'

Ross snorted. 'The police called Darcie yesterday to say that they'd spoken to Casey but, by the sounds of it, she'd just looked them in the eye and denied any involvement. There's no evidence, and gut feelings don't score points with the police.' He hadn't thought of a way to get back at Casey, yet, and that was irritating. He began to reverse the barrow. 'I'll go get the other four boxes.'

In a few minutes he returned with the second load. The shop area was deserted but he had been in the shop often enough to know where the stockroom was. He trucked his fragile load carefully past the glass shelves and propped the barrow upright outside the stockroom, hefted the top two boxes, groped at the handle with his elbow, pushed simultaneously with his shoulder and made his entrance.

Just in time to see his sister spring away from Jake Belfast so fast that she made the closed circuit TV monitor rock and Jake had to shoot out a steadying hand. Darcie's cheeks flamed.

Ross halted. Oh. Right. Fine. So, what? Was he supposed to pretend not to notice? He passed the boxes to Jake and went out for the others. Pausing for the door to swing shut behind him, he knocked loudly. 'Is it safe to come in this time?'

Darcie snatched the door open, redder than ever. 'Of course!'

He dropped the boxes into the waiting arms of a grinning Jake. 'You should tell me what's going on and then I would be more careful.'

Darcie glanced at Jake with a growing smile. 'It's all quite . . . new.'

Jake winked at Ross. 'Maybe for her.'

'You still could've told me.'

'She could,' Jake agreed, raising one eyebrow at Darcie.

Darcie met his gaze. 'And have you told Kelly?'

He grinned, suddenly. 'Now that you mention it . . . not yet.'

Darcie nodded, and moved the

conversation on to the new stock. Apart from casting the occasional glance at the closed circuit TV monitor, Jake seemed content to leave the shop to itself for a while, linking his fingers loosely through Darcie's.

Seemed like the kind of thing you ought to do with someone you liked. Not be pushed off all the time, like bloody Casey did . . .

On the TV monitor, Ross noticed a girl come into the shop, long dark hair hanging down her back, and thought for a frozen moment that he'd actually conjured Casey up from his thoughts. But, no — the girl turned around to face the camera and he saw that it wasn't her. Jake took a moment away from Darcie to watch, and check that the video tape was rolling but, picking up and putting down, the girl was obviously a browser rather than a shoplifter.

Ross stared at the black and white image of the girl leaving the shop, an idea forming at the edge of his mind, quickening his heart. 'Think I'll go down town,' he said, carelessly, before the idea could fade. 'I'll dump the barrow back in your workshop, Darcie.'

It was over a mile from the workshops to the town centre but Ross's long stride ate the distance. He wandered up and down High Street, in and out of shops, hands shoved in his pockets as he tried to find what he wanted. It took a little while, but then he found exactly the right place, Patsy's Emporium, the cool shop in town that played whale music and sold henna tattoos, scented candles and silver jewellery. It was exactly the kind of place Casey would hang out.

Even then, he couldn't really see exactly how to make his plan work without knowing more about what was happening with Casey. The school was alive with rumours, but he needed to know.

15

Darcie arrived home almost at the same time as Ross. She was glad to have the opportunity to talk to him alone. Jake's presence was disturbing on all kind of levels and trying to give Ross answers when she wasn't sure of them herself would feel like a special kind of awkward. 'Do you mind I didn't tell you about Jake?' she demanded, pulling off her jacket and hanging it over the newel post at the bottom of the stairs. They could do that now Mum wasn't there to sigh about it.

He shrugged. 'Just wondered why you hadn't.'

She gave him a quick hug. 'I suppose I didn't know what to tell you. There's something happening but I don't know what. It really just — '

'Happened?' he supplied. He gave her a quick squeeze before letting her go. 'Will you do me a favour?'

'Probably,' she agreed, cautiously, heart beginning to sink. Her relationship with Dean ending so soon after the loss of Mum and Dad, maybe Ross felt weird about something to do with Jake? She hadn't really done more than go out on the occasional date in the last couple of years and Ross hadn't had to deal with her love life. Maybe he was anticipating Jake staying the night. She could imagine him stigmatising it as 'gross' and —

'Would you ring Casey's mum?'

Her attention skipped awkwardly to the fresh subject. 'Why?'

He scowled. 'There are all these rumours at school about her being arrested but I don't even know whether she's coming back to school. Whether I've got to deal with her at some point. Nobody tells me. It's really getting to me.' He rubbed at the pattern on the carpet with his toe.

'Oh,' she said slowly. 'I suppose I could ask her. But her first reaction might be to tell me to go jump.'

'Yeah, OK. Thanks.' And, in the way of teenage boys, he launched himself suddenly at the bottom step and disappeared up to his room.

Darcie took a shower and blow-dried her hair, thinking about Ross's request. She wasn't totally on board with it, if she was honest with herself, but she'd do almost anything to help Ross. He'd had so much to deal with, losing Mum and Dad so young, and then, just when he seemed to be getting used to his new normality, being made a mug of by young Casey. It wasn't to be wondered at that the uncertainty of whether Casey was returning to school was playing on his mind, especially if she had been behind the attack on him.

Reluctantly, she went down to find the entry for Lynda McClare in the telephone directory, and dialled. 'I hope you don't resent this call,' she began.

Lynda, obviously a much nicer person than her daughter, made a sound that could have been a laugh, or a sob. 'I should imagine your family has more right to feel resentful than mine. Casey has behaved badly and your Ross is on my conscience — although he doesn't seem to be on Casey's; she's just lying around in her room as if the holidays have started early. They've allocated her a new school, but she won't go. Now the authorities are talking to me about a special educational unit but I suppose the truth is that she'll be sixteen in less than a year and past the age of compulsory education.' She drew in a wavering breath, before bursting out, 'I'm worried sick about her, if you want the truth.'

All antipathy dissolving in the face of such wretchedness, Darcie's heart melted, and even though Ross had padded downstairs when he heard her voice and had now propped himself against the door jamb to listen, she was sympathetic. 'I'm really sorry to hear that. I was trying to find out whether Casey would be returning to Rowlands for Ross's sake, but I hadn't really thought how horrible it must be for you. I expect Casey was arrested, was she, like Ross?'

'It was a nightmare. The police were quite nice, and we had a solicitor and everything, but they had all those phones as evidence and that friend of Ross's gave a statement that she sold his own phone back to him, so she was charged and we're waiting to hear when she goes to the Youth Court. The school doesn't want her back.'

'And what about Zoë?'

'Her! Never heard of again. Casey simply refuses to admit she ever existed and if I hadn't seen her with my own eyes I might even believe her. But,' she lowered her voice, 'I think Casey's pining for her. Waiting for her to get in touch. I suppose the woman's got more sense than that, though. Knows the police are interested in her.' She paused. 'And then I understand that Ross got roughed up? The police came to see Casey again, but she denied it was anything to do with her.'

'Well, there wasn't any evidence, was there?' said Darcie, diplomatically.

'No,' said Lynda. And sighed.

Darcie ended the call and filled Ross in on the details he hadn't been able to glean from her end of the conversation. He nodded, slowly. 'Thanks. I feel better, now I know she's being done. Nasty cow,' he added, venomously. 'Thanks, Darcie. I'm going to Jonny's, OK?'

★   ★   ★

Ross was soon knocking on Jonny's front door and saying hi to Jonny's mum, who knew him well enough to send him straight up to Jonny's room. 'Casey McClare wouldn't recognise your phone number, would she?' he asked, as soon as he'd settled on a corner of Jonny's bed to watch him play Super Mario Kart. Jonny was Donkey Kong, predictably enough, which meant he could only drive the heavy cars, barging everyone out of his way. Ross preferred Yoshi — still cool but you could select a medium weight car and use a bit of skill and finesse.

Jonny kept his eyes glued to his TV screen, his thumbs busy on his blue Wii controller and his black nunchuk. 'Nope. Never had more to do with her than I had to.'

'Can I use your phone to text her, then?'

'Why?' The thumbs moved faster and Jonny gave a little crow of delight as he barged a virulently coloured Bowser off the track.

'Piss her off.'

'OK.' A quick pause of the game for Jonny to dig his phone out of his pocket, then Jonny went back to racing virtual circuits, cursing quietly under his breath as he drifted wide at a corner, tyres sparking blue, whilst Ross took Casey's number from his own phone and began to text.

Its me. Got new phone number cops wont know. Z xxx

He watched Jonny's Donkey Kong get bounced over some rocks, the virtual tyres squealing as if in dismay.

Jonny never watched his power ups or where opponents were on his circuit map. He hoped this tournament was finished soon, so Jonny would go two-player with him, and Ross and Yoshi could kick his arse.

To his satisfaction, he had to wait only a minute for Casey's reply. She wasn't even cool enough to wait half an hour before replying.

Wicked lol r u OK xxxxxx

Fine thx r u?xxx This was really easy.

Yeh but my mum is a cow and cops r shit. im supposed to go to new school but not going. I didnt tell cops anythin lol

Love ya for that hun. Miss u. Can we meet up? R u grounded? xxx Ross grinned to himself to think of Casey receiving that and wondering how serious that *love ya* might be.

I can get out. want to meet ☺ Where? xxxxxxxxoxoxox

How bout tomorrow afternoon at 4 at patsys emporium. Round corner where crystals r so no one sees xxx

Yeh cant wait xxxxxoxoxoxo
☺ *Z x*

Ross dropped Jonny's phone on the bed and picked up another games controller, because Jonny's fourth level was just ending and they could go to multiplayer. 'If she texts your phone, forward it to me.'

Jonny just grunted, sighing in frustration as he was overtaken on the line, which pushed him back to fourth, off the podium.

★   ★   ★

It seemed like school would never end. Ross had to spend lunch and break wearing one of those loathsome yellow bibs and stuffing litter into black bin bags, then get his report card signed by his form teacher at the end of the day. Then he sprinted off into town, hiding himself in the cheap clothes shop opposite Patsy's Emporium and flicking through the same rack of jeans, over and over, waiting for Casey to appear.

Then, just when he thought she'd smelled a rat and wasn't going to turn up, she strode into view, hands stuffed in the pockets of a floor length black coat, hair flying. He gave her ten seconds after she'd disappeared into the shop, then sprinted after her, ducking through the door and flashing the woman behind the counter a smile as he made his way to the back of the shop past purple wizards, whose long thin wands were really incense sticks, and cases of vaguely gothic looking jewellery, following round to the right until he reached the place where crystals were displayed under pink spotlights.

And there Casey McClare stood, checking her phone.

'Hey,' he said softly, as he popped into her view.

She stared out from between artistic sweeps of eyeliner, glancing behind him.

'She's not coming.' He made himself as wide as possible, arms folded.

'What do you mean? What are you doing here?'

'I'm pretending to be Zoë, who has dumped your arse.' Ross grinned. 'Like I pretended last night by text. 'Love ya for that, hon,'' he quoted. 'You're such a loser, Casey. Mooning after some older babe who's been using you as a fence but letting you think she had feelings for you.'

Casey's dark eyes burned with anger and she stepped to her right as if to dodge around him. Ross easily moved left and blocked her in. 'Loser,' he taunted. 'Stupid little girl loser. You thought you were so fucking clever, didn't you? Trying to make a mug out of me? But I'm OK, Casey. The police let me off, because all the evidence pointed to you. Zoë got away by dumping you, knowing you were too in lurve with her to dob her in. Neither of us are going to court to get community service or crap. Neither of us have been kicked out of school and have to go to a special unit. It's just you, lost-your-girlfriend-Casey.' He stepped right, blocking her path again. 'Nothing bad happened to me. Just you.'

Casey halted, face a dull red of frustration. 'Yeah, right,' she sneered. 'Looks like nothing happened to you.' Her gaze ran contemptuously over his face. 'Black eye, split lip. But *nothing* happened to you.'

He smiled, smugly. 'Nothing to do with you, loser. Just some random guys who were looking for someone to give a kicking to.'

'Oh yeah?' She folded her arms. 'Oh *yeah*? It was at the end of Pebble Lane, wasn't it?'

His heart beat harder, his throat went dry. He let the smile drop from his face. 'How do you know that?'

Her eyes glittered with amusement. 'Who do you think set it up, following you around, just waiting to set them on you? Unsad Zag, my invisible gnome? Or my abusive dad or beaten-down mum? I know you're fucking gullible but I didn't think you were stupid.' Her eyes hardened. 'You dropped me right in the shit, you bastard, with your fucking statement. And Zoë. You could've got Zoë sent to jail. So I just thought I'd teach you a lesson.'

He made his voice ludicrous with dismay. 'You set those big guys on me?'

Throwing back her head, she laughed. 'I gave them thirty quid each to show you what's what. What do you think of that, then — *loser?* And if you fuck with me again I'll screw you up so tight your fucking eyes will roll out and explode. And then I'll rip your tongue out to clean up the mess.'

This time, Ross let her push past him. He smiled, a long, satisfied smile at the small black camera up in the corner, trained on the part of the shop that was out of sight of the person at the till. 'Gotcha, Casey McCatspaw. Bet you look really good on CCTV.' Ross laughed, even though it stung his stitches. 'Wicked.'

He took out his phone, which he'd had on voice recorder, just in case the camera failed to pick the conversation up, ended the recording, and rang his sister. 'Hey, Darcie. Have you still got the number of that policeman who dealt with me getting shoved down-stairs?'

16

Darcie settled her legs more comfortably over Jake's and her head against the wing of the sofa as she brought him up to date on Ross's adventures. Her behind was warm and round in his lap, a tingling place for it to be. She said, 'So we went to the station and Ross played the voice recording to the police officer and they're going to ask to see the video footage from Patsy's Emporium, so that they can see it was definitely Casey speaking. If it all works out, they expect to be interviewing her again, shortly.'

Jake smiled in satisfaction. 'He makes an implacable enemy, that little brother of yours. I've made a note to myself not to get on the wrong side of him in the future.'

Her eyes widened and she said, cautiously, 'You're almost speaking as if you expect to be around.'

He tried to read her expression. 'That depends on you. Us.' He lifted her hand from her lap and ran her fingertip lightly over his lips. 'We've made it past the day after hot sex, so we're doing better than last time. But you aren't involved with anyone else, which really helps.'

'I only needed a little bit of time to uninvolve myself, before,' she asserted, softly. 'You just didn't stick around to listen.'

Slowly, he nodded. Here it came. Time to face the truth. Just when it had looked as if the present was going to be a joyous ride, they were preparing to broach the future. He hoped reaching it wasn't going to hurt. 'OK. I'm listening, now.'

She took a deep breath. 'OK. Let's try it again. I went to see Dean, to end things with him. Before I could explain, he burst out that he was being made redundant. He was really upset because he'd just booked an expensive holiday and his car went with his job so he'd lose that, too. Even though I wanted to be with you, and even before . . . that night . . . I had realised that the end was near, I still cared about him. I knew I was going to find it difficult to hurt him, anyway, but to listen to his really bad news and then go, 'Oh, and guess what? I slept with Jake last night and I'm dumping you . . . ' ' She swallowed. 'I just couldn't. I thought you'd understand that I needed to give him a few days. But when I tried to tell you . . . '

His voice emerged on a croak. 'You're joking. I asked if you'd told him and you said, 'I care too much' — ?'

Her eyes burned into his. 'I was trying to say I cared too much to drop it on him at that moment. Dean hadn't done anything wrong and I would have had to be a super bitch to finish things whilst he was so upset. Next thing I knew, I was talking to your back as you stalked off.' Her smile was crooked. 'I decided that I'd give you a few days to get over yourself, and then make another attempt to explain. Before I could, Kelly came round all upset that you'd taken the job in Germany.'

That was another thing he'd never really understood. 'But you obviously never told Kel about that night. It was as if you were trying to forget it ever happened.'

She laughed, bitterly. 'Like, 'Oh, I had a hot night with your brother, but then he acted like a petulant kid, so it's already over'? I wasn't going to risk your macho pride making things difficult between me and Kelly. Especially as then . . . well, Mum and Dad were killed.' A tear eased from the corner of her eye and she brushed it away. 'And when you heard the news and rang — guess what? Dean had just told me that he couldn't see our relationship working with me moving back here to make a home for Ross, he didn't want to be tied down by his own kids for years to come, let alone by someone's teenage brother. So I wasn't in the mood to justify myself to you. Or to soothe your ego.'

Jake gazed at her wordlessly.

*   *   *

His expression of horror and dismay actually made Darcie laugh. It was so ludicrous. 'So that's why I said I could cope without you.'

'Shit,' he muttered, hoarsely.

'That's pretty much what I called you.' A sigh rose from deep inside. 'Now we're having this long-overdue heart-to-heart, you might as well understand that — well, I've got Ross. He might seem like almost an adult, but he's got three more years at school, and then he might go to uni.'

She pulled in a long, wavering breath, flicking a glance at him through spiky lashes. 'Ross isn't a commitment I pick up and put down. When I offered him a home it was a proper home, not a make-do. I promised him that, and that's what I'm going to give him.' She

195

gazed past his ear, waiting for him to consider, to temporise, explain that his job would probably take him away and all he wanted was something light.

Yeah. And maybe they'd have something light until he went. Why not? So long as it didn't affect Ross. The damage had already been done to her heart so she might as well get something out of allowing herself to open up to Jake — figuratively and literally — and fall in love. When the affair careered to its natural end, she'd just have to get herself all zipped closed again.

His hand tightened on hers. 'Darcie — '

And then her phone rang, cutting through the conversation as if it had planned it. When Darcie saw Lynda McClare's name on the screen, she sighed. 'Sorry, I have to take this. Hullo?'

Lynda McClare sounded annoyed. 'Look, Darcie,' she said, 'I know your lad's had a lot to put up with, and I know Casey's given him hell. But I'm afraid that if he pisses in my front porch again, I'll report him to the police.'

Darcie closed her eyes. Brilliant, Ross had picked his moment to start acting up. 'Oh no! I'll make sure that it doesn't happen again.'

But good. Good. *Good!* Better Jake should realise that this was what her commitment to Ross meant, the type of thing she had to deal with.

Her role was to be available when her little brother went pissing on doorsteps.

Unsteadily, she rang Ross. 'Lynda McClare says you just peed on her doorstep and she's talking about notifying the police.'

Silence.

'Did you?'

A heavy sigh. 'I was annoyed.'

Darcie's eyes prickled with fresh tears. 'That wasn't a wise thing to do. You'd got your revenge and your place was in the right. Why did you have to do something so stupid, and put yourself in the wrong?' A couple of the tears burned their way out from under her lids.

'I was just . . . Has she really set the police on me?'

'Not yet.'

'How does she know it's me?'

'I suppose she must have been watching.'

'Oh. Gross.' But there was a note of laughter in his voice.

The tears tipped from her eyes and dripped down both cheeks, making Darcie suffer a complete sense of humour failure. 'Where are you?'

'On the bench at the bottom of Queen's Road.'

'Come home, Ross. You're grounded.'

'I'm — ?' Disbelief was loud in his voice.

'Grounded,' she confirmed, wiping her face with her palm. 'Home in five.' And ended the call.

Her eyes felt like they'd been licked shut like an envelope. She eased herself from Jake's lap without looking at him and nipped up to the bathroom to repair the damage she'd done to her mascara, and didn't run back down the stairs until she heard Ross slam in through the door.

'This is so lame,' he said, belligerently. 'Casey — '

She cut him off with a glare. 'I don't care what Casey does. I care what Ross does. You either accept that you're grounded or you go along to the McClare's house and apologise, and wash up your mess.' She broke off to glare briefly past him to where Jake had suddenly begun to grin.

Horror flashed across Ross's face. 'Clean it up? But Casey would piss herself — '

'And that would make two of you!'

'All right,' he snapped. 'I'm grounded. But this is lame.' And he strode past her and up the stairs in three angry strides.

Jake hadn't moved from the sofa, although his eyes still danced. She dropped down beside him and closed her eyes. 'Don't laugh. That boy kills me.'

He placed his hand deliberately on her left breast. 'Your heart is still beating.' He stooped and kissed the same spot. Then he trailed his hand down to her waistband and began to flip open her jeans.

Ignoring a jolt of desire, she placed her hand over his. 'Sorry. Ross might come in. No can do.'

Slowly, he removed his hand, meeting her eyes. 'Wow. This is a real test isn't it? I could completely screw everything up with the wrong reaction.'

She shrugged. 'It's not a test. It's real life. It's what happens around Ross. He gets in scrapes, he comes over all teenager. He gets moody when he's dealing with his grief for Mum and Dad. If you're not happy with that . . . '

He lifted his hand to her cheek. 'I could be ecstatically happy — with Ross around — if you want me.' He moved his finger to her lips to halt her impetuous interruption. He stared into her eyes. 'See, if you *want* me, if you want us to be together, I want it, too. Ross is a great kid. I'll find another job in this area and do my damnedest to give us all a happy ever after.

'What I can't do is stay, watching you, wanting you, if you don't want it to work out. I couldn't do it before, and I can't do it now.'

Darcie felt joy begin to seep into all her limbs, like the effects of a drug. She slid her fingertips into his waistband and let them brush against warm, hairy flesh. 'And if I don't want it to work out, would you get up all indignant and tell me to keep my clothes on?'

He began to smile. 'No.' He shifted a little as her fingers probed. 'Are you going to say that?'

'No,' she whispered, biting gently at his throat, tasting the saltiness of his skin. 'I want you very much. I want you now, this instant, I want you to stay and I want to be together. Most of all, I want you to love me. So that it's OK to love you.' She gasped as her fingertip brushed the silken heat of him.

'I do love you,' he whispered, touching her lips with the tip of his tongue. 'And I want you very very much. I want you hot and naked. But,' he unhooked her fingers out of the top of his jeans, 'behave yourself. Ross might come in.' He winked.

Shocked at herself at such a lapse, she froze. Wow, she'd almost got completely carried away with Jake's heat and nearness.

Then she relaxed, giving him her hottest, sexiest smile. 'But he's the one who's grounded. We're not. Your place?'